All characters in this publication are fictitious and persons, living or dead is purely coincidental.

CW01494983

Liar

by

Seán Hogan

Where's Your Dad?

"Why don't you have a dad?"

"I do have a dad, he's just busy. He's going to come here one day and I'll bring him to school and then you'll all stop laughing at me. He's big and tall, if you laugh at me he'll beat you all up."

I turn and run away to the sounds of laughter and my classmates copying my voice. It doesn't happen all the time, only sometimes. When they are bored and want to pick on someone different they choose me. The rest of the time it's the fat kid whose clothes don't fit him properly. I'm thankful for the fat kid. If it wasn't for him it would be me all the time. I hope he never goes on a diet or his mum never wins money. I sit in the corner of the playground, watching and waiting until they forget they were picking on me.

They're right, I don't have a dad. I have never seen him, I don't even know what his name is. I don't want to admit that to them though. If I admitted it then they would tease me more. If I lie it might make them think, maybe some of them will believe me and be scared. Mum says I shouldn't listen to what the other kids say. She says they are only jealous of me because I can tell such good stories. None of them want to listen to my stories though. If they only listened for ten minutes they would like them, they would stop teasing me then.

I hope mum hasn't gone out tonight. I have a new story I want to tell her. She hasn't been home in the evenings for weeks, when she gets back I'm already in bed asleep. I know we need the money but she spends it all anyway. If she isn't home tonight I'll just go and see the nice old lady, Mrs Smith that lives in the block next door. I wanted mum to be the first to hear it but I just can't keep it in anymore, if I don't tell someone I'll forget it. The other kids have started to tease the fat kid. I think it's safe to go back out to the playground.

As I walk towards them I kick a stone that's lying on the floor. Pretending to be a football player. Pretending I'm at Wembley and about to score a goal in the cup final. One of the other kids comes over and joins me. He's not my friend but he doesn't tease me. He talks to me about football and what he does at the weekend. If none of the other kids see him, he sometimes walks home with me after school. He lives on the floor above me. He said his mum doesn't want him to walk back with me but he doesn't care. Just don't let her see us together.

As we kick the stone to each other he asks me what I'm doing after school tonight. I tell him I need to go home and see my mum because she's been busy working recently. I can see a smirk on his face as I say it. One of the other kids calls out to him and he runs off, leaving me to the stone and my imagination. The teacher told Mrs Smith I have a vivid imagination. Mum was busy so she couldn't go to the parents' evening. Mrs Smith said she would go instead. I don't really know what a vivid imagination is. I do like to dream though, even when I'm awake I still try to dream.

Back in the classroom the teacher gives us some work. It's boring. I wish she would give us something exciting to do. If she gave us something interesting she wouldn't have to tell me off for daydreaming. I look around the classroom at all the other kids. Some of them are sleeping and some of them are doing their work. The teacher isn't paying any attention. The fat kid is playing with his ruler. I sometimes wonder if one day he'll go crazy and kill us all. I hope he doesn't, maybe I should make friends with him. Then he might not kill me, just kill all the others.

The bell rings and the teacher lets us go. I run out the door as fast as I can, the quicker I get out the further away I am from the kids that walk the same way home as me. I look back and can't see any of them. I walk slower, if I get home too quickly mum might not be there, the later I am, the more chance there is she'll be home. I wish she would take a holiday like some of the other kid's mums. I don't think she has ever taken a holiday. As I walk across the park I can see our estate, I can even see our flat's windows. It doesn't look like anyone is home, just by looking at the windows I know if someone is inside or not.

Our estate is big. Big, tall, long buildings. We live on the bottom floor so I can play football outside the door if mum is at home and busy with work. There are ten floors above us. I always wanted to live on one of the higher floors, if I lived on one of them I could look out across the city. I can't see anything from my window, only trees. The boy in my class who lives above me said at night you can see all the lights from the other buildings. I asked him if I could come up and see it sometime but he said his mum doesn't allow anyone inside their house.

There is a park just outside the door too. We don't use it though. At night some of the older kids hang around there smoking and drinking. There is broken glass all over the floor. One of the little girls that lives next to Mrs

Smith went in there one day and her hand got pricked by a needle. They had to take her to hospital. Mrs Smith said the needle could make her very sick. She has to wait for three months before she knows if she's okay. Now none of the other children will play with her. Even my mum said don't play with her and my mum doesn't care who I play with.

Next to the park there is a newspaper shop, an off license and a fish and chip shop. Sometimes when mum has some money she lets me go to the fish and chip shop to buy dinner. I buy a battered sausage and a large portion of chips. If I have enough money I buy a coke too. Mum sends me to the newspaper shop to buy her cigarettes, I'm supposed to be 16 to buy them but the man doesn't care, he knows they are for mum. When he gives me the cigarettes he winks at me. I feel bad because sometimes I steal a chocolate bar when he turns around to get the cigarettes.

I've only been into the off license once. They only sell beer in there and the man wouldn't let me buy it for mum. He said if she wants it she'll have to come and get it herself. I know he sells it to the other kids though. I see them at night when I'm kicking the ball against the wall. I'm not sure why he doesn't like me. After that day I went home and wrote a story about the man and he got eaten by a lion. I told it to mum and she really liked that one. I hope she likes my new one, it doesn't have any lions but it has a dinosaur. Mrs Smith will definitely like it.

Our flat is right in the middle of the block. There are nineteen flats on our floor and ours is number 9. Last year mum stopped working for a few months. She said she needed a rest. She painted the door red and put some flowers on the window ledge. When she went back to work I tried to keep the flowers alive but they died. I gave them water every day but it didn't seem to work. The door is dirty now too, one of the windows has some cardboard in the corner, someone threw a stone at it. I don't know why. I remember it frightened me. Mum said not to worry, it was an accident, I'm not sure it was though.

I open the door and call out. There's no reply. The house is empty. I look into mum's room to see if she has been home recently. Her clothes are all over the floor and I can smell her perfume. Her room is different from the rest of the flat. The walls are a dark pink colour. There is carpet on the floor too. It's clean, the clothes just making it look messy. There are mirrors on the wall and she has a lamp on the table next to her bed. I'm not allowed to go in there but when she's out I always open the door to have a look.

The living room doesn't have much in it. There is one sofa, a wooden chair in the corner and a small table with a tele on top. We used to have a coffee table in the middle but it disappeared one day. Mum said she threw it out because she didn't like it but I looked in the rubbish tip outside and couldn't see it. Maybe someone came and took it away. The floor has no carpet, only black tiles that are freezing cold in the winter, especially if she forgets to pay the electricity bill. Last year when she forgot I could see my breath in the air. I took some sheets from my bed and pretended I was on an expedition to the Antarctic to find some penguins.

My room is the smallest. I have my bed and a small wardrobe to keep my clothes in. There is no carpet in my room either. The walls are painted white, I want to paint them blue but mum says I'll have to wait until next year. Underneath my bed I keep some of the books I stole from the library. I push them right into the corner so that she can't find them. Not that she comes in here anyway. Just in case, though. If she found out I was stealing books she would never let me go to the library again.

It's nearly summer time so the house isn't very cold. It doesn't get dark until very late either. When it doesn't get dark until late I can stay outside playing football for longer. I can stay at Mrs Smith's for longer too. She doesn't like me to walk home in the dark on my own. I'm not scared but she says some of the older kids might cause trouble and she is too old to walk home with me because she'd have to walk back on her own then. I think she doesn't want to see mum, but maybe she's right, it isn't very safe around here at night.

Looking out the window I see some of the other kids playing football. I really want to go out and play with them but they won't let me. They call me names and say bad things about my mum. Instead I just watch them from the window, hoping they can't see me. Every time I watch them playing I hope they will stop playing and call out to me to come and join them. I can show them how good I am then, I could even tell them about myself, if they knew about me they wouldn't hate me anymore.

It starts to get dark, their mums' call out to them from the windows above, none of them wanting to hurry inside. If it was my mum calling me I would come in as quick as I could. They don't seem to care though, they see their mums all the time. I only see mine when she isn't busy at work and that's not often. When they've gone back inside, I think about sneaking upstairs to one of the balconies, and looking out over the city. I hear a loud bang from outside, one of the older kids is playing with a firework. I change my mind.

I think about the presentation we have to do at school tomorrow. We have to think of a place we'd really like to go to and describe it to the rest of the class. I still can't think of somewhere that I'd really like to go to. The teacher says it has to be real, I can't make it up. One of the books I stole from the library is the Jungle Book. I'm not sure if it's real or not. Mrs Smith said it's in India but I don't believe there are animals that can talk in India. I think I will choose the jungle in India, I just won't talk about animals that talk, I can have animals though, especially tigers, I love tigers.

I don't know what the jungle looks like, I can only think of it as how I imagine. I close my eyes and pretend I'm there in India. I can see really tall trees, the top is completely green, and the sky is covered by the leaves with only small bits of light coming through. It's hot, really hot. I'm wearing only a t-shirt and some shorts. Above me I can see monkeys swinging through the trees, screaming out loudly, telling all the other monkeys there is a small nine year old boy walking through their jungle. They hold their babies close to their bodies as they swing through the trees.

In front of me there is a river. I can see a crocodile waiting, patiently waiting for something to come along that it can eat. A small deer is next to the river drinking water. The top of the crocodile moves along the surface silently, the deer can't to see or hear him. As the crocodile sneaks up on the deer one of the monkeys lets out a loud screech and the deer turns and runs back into the green forest. The crocodile is angry that he has to wait longer to have his dinner. The monkeys laughing to themselves, they've ruined the crocodile's plans.

Across the river I spot a tiger. She moves slowly through the forest, frightened of nothing. The monkeys stop laughing and swing back through the trees. The master of the forest has arrived and everyone is making way. From across the river she spots me, only looking quickly before carrying on her way. Not bothered about the small boy walking through her home. Maybe she thinks I'm not enough to eat, she wants something bigger. Even the crocodile has swum away. Away from the beautiful cat to find somewhere he can wait in peace, away from the monkeys too.

As the tiger walks off to find her dinner a large bird flies down from the trees and perches on a branch next to my head. A parrot. He looks at me, his look asking what am I doing here. Am I lost? I shake my head in reply. He lets out a loud squawk and flies away again. It is so peaceful here. Only the sounds of the animals and the water flowing. I'm in a place where nobody can tease me. I wish I could wait here all the time, every evening I spend on my own waiting for mum to come home I wish it was here in this forest.

I jump to another loud bang. This time it's not a firework but the sound of the door closing. It has gotten dark without me noticing, mum has arrived home. I haven't turned any of the lights on so she probably thinks I'm asleep. Her footsteps sound clumsy, as though she is tripping over. I know she isn't wearing her high heels because I saw them on the floor when I looked in her room. She goes into the kitchen and I hear the sound of her lighter. The same sound for the next ten minutes click, click, click. I quickly take off my clothes and get underneath the covers of my bed, hoping the door will open just a crack and she'll look in.

Another twenty minutes pass and there is still no sound from the kitchen. Maybe she's tired, sometimes she falls asleep on the kitchen table. I hear the sound of the chair moving against the floor and my heart jumps. Her footsteps get closer to my door and then stop just outside. The door opens slightly and I can just see her face. She is smiling, but her hands are shaky, the door wobbling slightly back and forth. I pretend to be asleep. I'm annoyed that she didn't come home in time for me to read my story.

She closes the door quietly. I hear her footsteps go into her own room, the sound of her falling onto her bed. Tonight she is back early, I hope she will be awake in the morning. I want to tell her to take some time off, she looks tired lately. She won't listen to me but I can try. I drift off to sleep, flying back to the jungle that is my new safe place, where the animals won't tease me or eat me. Where I don't have to wait each night for mum to come home. Where I don't have to pretend I have a dad.

I've Made Mistakes

I've let him down, I know that. When I look in at him at night I know he's still awake, I can't bring myself to talk to him, what am I supposed say to him? I don't think he's as innocent as he makes himself out to be, surely he must know what's going on. The kids at his school, I knew all their mums when I was at school, they like to talk, but what else can I do? I can't take him out of school, he can't be hanging around here all day. Anyway, I want him to be at school, I want him to do well for himself, I can't have him ending up like me.

I'm getting more and more tired of all of this. Standing around on lonely street corners every night, when it's all finished going to some manky old squat and then coming back home. What kind of life is it? If I was on my own I reckon I'd just end it all, but I couldn't do that to him, I might not give him the best life but it would be better than the life he'd have in some home or with some family that don't really care about him. I've tried to get out of this circle before but I always fail, I don't know how to live any other way.

The road is dark, next to the old canal, the streetlights aren't all working, I'm used to it, and I've forgotten what it feels like to be scared. Well scared like most people think, you know? Scared of being murdered or raped, I don't ever get scared like that no more. What's the point? If I was I might as well stay at home and then we definitely wouldn't have anything to eat. When I say I'm scared, I'm scared of myself, scared of what I'm doing to myself, scared of what I'm doing to the boy, how is this all going to affect him when he's older?

At the end of the dark road I turn onto the high street, there ain't anyone about at this time of the night apart from a couple of homeless old boys. I suppose it could be worse, I could be one of them. I have something I can hold on to. The walk back every night is the worst part, the shame is all over me, my body constantly feels dirty, and sometimes I walk back slower, just to make sure he's not awake to see me come in the door. I know that's what he wants, but I can't face him, it's too difficult.

If his dad had stayed around I wonder if it would've all turned out like this. I doubt it, I wouldn't have to do what I do. It was all different when he was around. He looked after me, I've never been able to look after myself. He would've looked after the boy too, the day he walked out, it was the day that led us to this. I still don't blame him, I can't, he didn't know what to do, he couldn't handle it all, he was scared and he ran, if I had the choice at the time I think I would've ran too. I didn't have that choice though, I had to stay.

I remember looking into his big blue eyes as he lay in my lap. I knew I couldn't leave him, I couldn't give him to no one else. I promised myself that day I would do the best I could for him, try to give him the best life I possibly can, it ain't really worked out like that, I'm still trying but I'm starting to give up hope that things will ever work out the way I wanted them to. People will probably say it's my own fault, it's because I'm selfish, but I don't know any other way to handle life. I was too young, they don't

15

think about that though do they? They just want to put you down all the time.

There's a couple of kids in the park, not sure what they are doing but it's probably not something good at this time of night. I know some of them go in there to do gear. When I see them I want to shake them, I want to ask them what the fuck do they think they're doing, why are they wasting their lives going down the same fucking road I went down? They probably think it's one of them roads where you can just turn around and walk back, but it ain't, it's nothing like that, it's a long straight road where a brick wall follows right behind you.

The house is quiet, he must have gone to bed because none of the lights are on. I wonder what he does in the evening? I don't ask because it makes me feel even guiltier. It's always so fucking cold in here, I really must buy us a heater so he can keep warm at night, I meant to buy one last week but I forgot. I sit down at the kitchen table and smoke a cigarette, and another one. I'm starting to feel sick, the goose pimples rising on my skin. I'll wait until I'm in my room though, it feels better when you tease yourself, it's the one rule I have as well, only in my room.

I stand up and look at the small mirror that's on the kitchen wall. My eyes are dark, my face skinny and pale even with make up on I look ill. How must he feel to have this come home to him every single night? I light another cigarette and sit down, I'll take that mirror down in the morning, I don't want to have to keep looking at myself when I get in. One last cigarette before I go and check on him, I have to smoke at least three, I'm nervous, I keep waiting for the day where he isn't there when I get home, that he's had enough and run away.

I look through the crack in the door, he looks asleep but I'm sure he's awake. There's a smile on his face, he knows I'm here. I'm feeling a bit shaky so I hold on to the door handle, I don't want to walk away just yet. I can't believe that such a complete waste of a fucking life like me could have created something as beautiful as him. I don't know where he got his intelligence from either, I doubt it was from me, well it can't have been. I kiss my finger tips and blow it towards him, smile and walk to my room, the sickness is coming fast and I need to stop it.

New Friend

The bell rings and we all rush outside. The fat kid following behind, trying to be one of us, well one of them, I'm not one of them either. He trips on a schoolbag that has fallen on the ground. I want to go and help him up, I wait until nobody else can see. Just him and me. I reach out my hand to him, he looks up surprised that I'm there helping him. He brushes my hand away but smiles as he stands up. He pulls a biscuit out of his trouser pocket and gives it to me. I hope it hasn't been in his pocket for very long.

We walk in silence together to the wall on the far side of the playground. We walk past the other kids teasing a little girl because her shoes are old. We look at each other and smile, happy it's neither of us. As we sit down on the wall he gives me another biscuit. I still haven't finished the first one. If he becomes my friend, does it mean I'm going to be fat like him? I hope not. My mum said fat people die young. Mrs Smith said he's probably just big boned, but he doesn't look like he has big bones. To me he just looks fat.

"I've seen you on our estate, why don't you go out and play?"

"I don't feel like it. I stay at home and read my books."

"Books are boring! I don't go out either. The other kids on the estate make fun of me. Last time I went to play with them they threw me into the rubbish bin. My mum said I should hit them, but I don't like fighting. I like to stay at home and play with my computer games."

I wonder how many of them it took to throw him in the rubbish bin. The bins on our estate are quite tall. They must have been really strong.

"You can come to my house if you want." The way he looks at me is weird.

"No it's okay, my mum says your mum is a bad lady. You can come to my house though, my mum said you look like a nice kid, shame about your mum though."

"Your mum doesn't know my mum."

"I know, but my mum talks about everyone. I wouldn't worry about it. If you come she'll give you lots of sweets."

"Okay, I'll ask my mum if I can go at the weekend. I'll let you know tomorrow."

The bell rings and we go back to class for the last part of the day. I did my presentation this morning. The teacher said it was excellent. The other kids laughed, they said it was stupid. I don't really car, I know some of them enjoyed it because they were quiet while I was telling it to them. They only laughed after because the naughty kids did. None of their presentations were exciting anyway. They all wanted to go to stupid places like the park or a football match. At least mine was more interesting than theirs.

When it's time to go home I don't rush out the door like everyone else. I wait for the fat kid to catch up with me. We walk home together. Every time he reaches in to his pocket I think he's going to give me another biscuit. As we walk past the park he says we should go and play in the small woods for a little while. I know mum won't be at home so she won't worry. I've stopped hoping she'll be at home now. Her looking in at me when she comes home is enough. I know one day she'll stop working and we can spend all our time together. Maybe if she has enough money I won't have to go to school.

Me and my new friend walk into the woods. Mrs Smith has told me I shouldn't go in here, there might be bad men who will take me away. It doesn't look like there are any bad men in here though. Just rubbish, old magazines and washing machines. We kick the washing machines and I try to climb a tree. He just watches me, knowing he wouldn't be able to do it himself.

"Where's your dad?"

"Why?"

"My mum says you've got lots of dads. The other kids say you haven't got one..."

From anyone else this question would upset me. He doesn't look like he is being nasty though.

"My dad is a singer..."

"What!?"

"Yeah, he's a singer but you can't tell anyone. It's a secret. I'm not supposed to tell anybody either but I'll tell you because you're my friend. If you do tell anyone I won't be your friend no more."

"Why is your dad being a singer a secret? I wish my dad was a singer. He only sits around all day drinking beer. He sings but he can't sing. Mum hits him when he sings because she says he sounds like a baby cat drowning."

"It's a secret because my mum doesn't want anyone to know. Dad doesn't either, he says if people know they would ask him for money. He lives in Spain on the beach. He has a big house too. Please don't tell anyone."

"I promise, as long as I can meet him! If your dad is a singer why do you live here? I thought singers were rich. You could live anywhere you wanted to."

"When he comes back we'll go and live in a big house far away from here. He is saving his money at, we don't mind living here because we know when he comes back we'll be rich."

"Can I come and see your big house?"

"Of course you can."

"You should tell your dad about those kids at school. He'd stop them teasing you, he could stop them teasing me as well now we're friends. If they knew your dad was famous they wouldn't tease you."

"He isn't that famous. I can't tell them because they will tell everyone and dad doesn't want anyone to know."

"I suppose. I have to go home now or my mum will shout at me for missing my tea. I'm hungry anyway. Don't forget to ask your mum if you can come to my house at the weekend. I will ask my mum when I get home."

He runs off ahead of me worried his mum won't give him his dinner. I didn't think he could move that fast. I wonder if he really believes me. I've never told a lie like that before. I like to tell stories but I don't usually lie. If mum knew I was lying she would kill me. I don't really feel bad though. Maybe a little bit. I feel excited, I have a new friend and he likes me. When I told him my dad was a singer his eyes grew rounder. He was excited! A small lie can't hurt if it helps me make some new friends. I won't do it again though, just the once.

Walking in the door I can tell mum has left recently. If I hadn't gone to the woods I would've been able to see her. I'd have been able to tell her my story quickly. I'm not going to tell Mrs Smith, I'm going to wait until I have the chance to tell mum. The smell of her perfume is still just inside the door. I go to her room quickly, forgetting to shut the door. There is nobody there. On the floor is a piece of shiny paper with brown marks on it. I pick it up and sniff it. It smells sweet. She must have bought dinner from somewhere and wrapped it in foil. Her room smells sweet too, I feel a little bit sick from the smell.

I'm worried she was waiting for me to come home. I hope she'll wait again tomorrow. Usually I would be sad, once I cried when I just missed her. This time I know I have a new friend. If he doesn't tell his mum where he is going he can come here some evenings. I didn't ask him if he likes stories but he said he doesn't like books. I don't understand how anyone can't like books. Oh well, he must like something that I like. He doesn't tease me either. I'm not sure why his mum doesn't like my mum though. Why does she think I have lots of dads? I don't have any dad. Maybe she went to school with my mum, that's how they know each other.

I go to the fridge to see if there's anything in there to eat but there isn't anything. Completely empty, apart from some milk but it smells. I'll have to go out and buy something for my dinner. I could go to the chip shop. I know where mum keeps some of her money, I can take some. I don't think she notices, she doesn't say anything anyway. I'll only take enough to get some chips and a battered sausage, my favourite. The man in the chip shop is nice too. He talks to me when I go in there. Doesn't ask me about my mum either.

I take £5 from her drawer. I notice there are see little white stones in there too, they look like sweets. I was going to eat one but thought I had better not before dinner. I love the smell of the chip shop. It makes me feel all warm, especially in the evenings when it gets cold. The man who owns it is a big Greek man. Every time I go in he tells me I should wear more clothes, it is too cold just to be wearing a sweater. He shivers as he looks at me, turns away and mutters something in his language. This time he goes to the fridge and takes out a Coke, he hands it over to me and winks "No money" and then laughs that crazy laugh he has.

I sit down on the chair to drink my coke before ordering my food. His shop is small, only enough for three or four people. Two chairs on one side for people who have to wait for their food.

"What you been up to today, young man? This time you have smile, I think you are happy?"

"Not much, just went to school then went to the woods after."

"Why you go to them woods on your own? It's dangerous. There could be ghosts in there" He laughs as he says it. Ghosts don't really bother me, I'm more worried about the bad men, I don't believe in ghosts!

"I went with my new friend, I helped him today at school and now he wants me to go to his house this weekend."

"Who your new friend?" he says, raising his eyebrows.

"He lives over there with his mum, I say, pointing to the block of flats through the window. His mum stands on the balcony during the day smoking and shouting."

"That fat kid? Every day he come here to buy chips. I don't think his mother knows. You be careful, his mother is not a nice lady. She talk too much. The kids at school still bother you?"

"Not really, yesterday a little bit but today they left me alone. I told you before it's no problem."

"If it's no problem why you tell me? You just be careful, you stay at school and study, them kids they will stay here all their lives. No job, ten kids, drinking, smoking, eating."

"They buy your fish and chips though."

"I tell you before don't be cheeky. Sometimes I think you grow up too fast. Your mind is very quick for a small boy. Now what you want? I have things to do."

He always says he has 'things to do' when he wants me to go. I know he likes talking to me though. I finish my coke as he wraps up my chips and battered sausage. I love the smell of the newspaper he uses to wrap up the chips. On the way back home I pass three of the older kids sitting on a wall. They all stare at me as I walk past. I look down at the floor, I don't look at them, if I look at them they'll start trouble.

"Tell your mum I'll be round later, I want a freebie though."

I keep walking, not looking back. I don't know what he means but I can still hear them laughing, whatever it was he meant they all thought it was funny. My mum doesn't know them either. So many people that don't know her but talk about her. I put the key into the door but it pushes open without me having to turn it. My heart skips, mum must be home! I run into the kitchen to find her sitting there with a man I've never seen before.

"Go and sit in the living room, sweetheart, eat your dinner. I'll be in in a minute. My friend is just leaving, we'll just finish this coffee."

I look over at the man sitting by the table. He's a big man. He doesn't look very friendly, I smile at him but he doesn't smile back. I leave the kitchen quickly, still excited that mum is home, just waiting for this strange man to leave. I hope he leaves soon, I have a bad feeling about him. I can tell mum doesn't like him, she looks a frightened.

"Don't forget what I said, don't fuck me around this time. I'm not playing anymore." I hear the man say as he leaves. He slams the door. She doesn't come in straight away, I guess she's just standing by the door. I don't want to go out to her in case I upset her. She doesn't like me disturbing her when she's quiet. I try to eat my dinner but I'm too excited, not scared now the man has left. I hear her heels walking into her room and then a

25

rustling noise. Another ten minutes later she comes out. She looks tired, underneath her eyes are black. She smiles as she comes into the room holding out her arms. I get up and run to her, holding and not wanting to let go.

"Sit down and finish, your dinner. I'm not going out again tonight, don't worry."

"Who was that man?"

"He's just one of my friends. You won't see him again."

"I don't think he's very nice."

"He's okay, don't worry about him. How has school been? You're always asleep when I come in."

"It's okay. It's a bit boring, I think it's too easy. Today I told the teacher and the rest of the class about a place I want to go to. I talked about the jungle. The teacher said it was excellent! Oh, and I made a new friend today too, I think you would like him. Can I go to his house on Saturday?"

"Who is he?"

"You know that fat lady that stands on the balcony on the block over there? She's always shouting. That's his mum."

"Oh God. You can go if you like but just don't answer any questions she asks you. Especially about me. She's a nosy cow and I don't want her talking about us. She tells the whole estate everybody's business."

"Okay, I won't. He seems nice though."

"I'm sure he is love. I'm glad your little story went well too. You'll have to tell it to me sometime."

"I want to but you're never here, mum"

"I know love, but I have had to try and make some money for us to be able to eat. That fiver you took out of my drawer to buy your dinner, where do you think that came from?"

I look down at my dinner as she says this. I thought she never knew.

"I don't mind you taking it sometimes. Just don't do it all the time. I don't have much at the moment. Don't eat the sweets that are in there either. They're not for children, only adults can eat them."

Sometimes she treats me like I'm a grown up and sometimes like I'm a baby. I don't mind though, it's just good to have her home.

"Can I tell you a story tonight?"

"Not tonight, I'm really tired and I'm going to bed soon. I have some good news though. I'm going to take a holiday for two weeks. I'll be at home all day. When my holiday is over I'll be working from home. You can see me more that way."

I can't hold myself back from jumping back into her arms as she sits next to me. Finally we will be able to have time together.

"Mum..."

"Yes..."

"What do you do? I know you help people but what is your job?"

"I'm a special nurse, sweetheart. I help men with their problems. Some of them will have to come here so I can help them. They won't be here for long though. When they are here you can't disturb me."

I only care that she'll be home, I don't care who else will be here. Today is one of the best days of my life. I made a friend, mum is going to be around more and the teacher loved my story.

Tired Teacher

It's strange sitting in the classroom in the evenings. I've done this for so many years but without the kids in here it always feels odd. It's the noise that makes a school feel like a school, even when they're quiet, it feels as though noise cold erupt at any moment. My husband thinks I'm mad staying behind every evening to mark work, I can't do it at home though, I'd much rather finish it here and then go home and relax. I'd better get back to finishing off marking these presentations or I might as well sleep here for the night as I'll never get them finished.

Jay's was excellent when he was speaking about it in front of the class. It's so good to have a kid that has imagination. The stories he comes up with in the presentations that I set them are just incredible. You just know when a child has talent and can go places. I do worry that he won't fulfil his potential though, it's always the problem. I've been teaching here for 25 years and the number of times I've thought 'this kid really has it, he's going to go places' and then you see them a few years later and they're different people. I love teaching the younger kids, they still have that innocence and passion to learn new things.

I'm trying to think of ways that I can encourage him, I would speak to his mother but I have never met her. At parents' evening he always comes with another older lady who he says is his grandmother. I know the other kids tease him because he's so quiet, they tease him about his mother too. Apparently she's not in a very good way. I don't want to judge though, the poor kid, whatever is happening at home shouldn't stop him from doing something academically. He's always here though and he doesn't seem too unhappy.

I hate it when I hear some of the other teachers say things like 'most of them don't stand a chance anyway, look at where they are growing up, look at their families'. Surely it's our responsibility to try and give them some stability here? What does it matter where they grew up anyway? It's not half as bad as people say it is, that estate. It's no wonder most of them don't bother once they get into secondary school, they're pretty much told that they aren't going to achieve anything anyway. I'm sure that it's filled with untapped potential. A lot of those teachers at the secondary school just can't be bothered to make the effort.

They all say I'm an idealist, that I don't understand, if I really knew them I wouldn't be so passionate about helping the kids when they're at school. Yet, I'm the one who has been here for 25 years, I'm the only one who does actually know anything. I even had one kid come back to see me last week, he's not a kid anymore now, he went to university, he came back to the school to thank me. He said I was the one that started him on his journey to get where he is today. It's people like him who keep me doing what I am doing. I just wish I wouldn't get so attached sometimes, it hurts more when you see them give up on school.

That's the frustrating thing with this kid, I just can't really talk to him. I'm not sure that anything gets through. He'll nod his head and he'll agree with me but I can't get anything else out of him. I know he's shy but even when it's just the two of us he still barely speaks. It's like there's a barrier and he won't let me through it. The only person I have ever seen him really comfortable with was at parents' evening when he was with his grandmother. He isn't even naughty, he's never done anything bad in the classroom and he treats all the other kids with respect even though they don't seem to respect him.

I worry about him going to secondary school. At least here in primary school you can keep more of an eye on the kids, but when they move up it's more difficult. Kids at that age can be cruel. I'm not sure he even has any friends, I have seen him talking to Joe for the last few days though which is a good sign.

They've Got Carpets

Joe's house is nice. They've got a big tele in the living room, he's got computer games as well. There's two big sofas and a thick carpet on the floor. I keep looking around the room but don't want him to see. He might think I'm a bit weird. Their house feels so much warmer than ours. His sister is noisy though, always shouting at Joe, telling him he's fat and she wished he wasn't her brother. Joe just laughs and swears at her. His mum doesn't seem to take any notice. I thought she'd be angry at him. His dad talks to us about football and watches while we play games.

His mum asks me if I want to stay for dinner. She says I should call my mum and tell her, I say it's okay. I don't want them to know we don't have a phone. Mum is out anyway. She went out with some man, said she'd be back this evening sometime. She reminded me not to answer 'that nosey cow's' questions. She hasn't asked me any and I think she seems quite nice. She keeps asking me if I want another drink or if I'm hungry. It feels a bit strange, someone asking me if I want things all the time.

While we are playing games Joe's dad says he's going to a football match next weekend. If I want to come with him and Joe I can. I want to go, but I don't want to go either. I like being his friend and I like his family too, but I feel jealous. I know I shouldn't, but I wish I had a dad like that. I wish I had a dad. I feel sad, even when Joe's sister is shouting at him, at least he has someone that shouts at him. When I was small and mum left me on my own I used to pretend I had a big sister who would look after me. I'd pretend she took me out to places and sometimes shouted at me when I was naughty.

Joe's mum is sitting in the living room with us now. She keeps picking up cushions and throwing them at Joe, he laughs and throws them back. I thought his mum was really strict but she likes to play. She tells Joe they're going on holiday to the seaside this year. He doesn't seem too happy, he says they go there every year. I wish I could go to the seaside, just once. I've never even been outside the city. I'm angry at Joe because he doesn't want to go. I kind of feel I wish I hadn't come now because I'm happy and sad all at the same time.

"How's your mum? She working much lately?"

"She's okay, she's not working as much as she used. She works from home now most of the time. She's a special nurse so the people can come to our house."

She gives me a funny look, like I'm stupid, but I can see her eyes are sad too. I should ask her how she knows my mum.

"Anytime you want to come round here you can, when your mums got cust...patients you can come here and play with Joe. Even if Joe isn't here you can come round if you like. You can play with his games. Can't he Phil?"

"Course he can." Joe's dad smiles at me as he nods, "Anytime you like, mate."

I don't answer, I just nod my head. I want to say something but it won't come out. I feel a bit funny too. I think I prefer Mrs Smith's house. She talks to me like I'm a grown up. She doesn't talk about my mum either. I'm trying to ask her how she knows my mum but I can't. It's like I'm too scared to talk, it's the same when some of the big kids say things to me. She just smiles and walks back out to the kitchen. Joe doesn't take any notice. He's concentrating too much on his game. I used to feel sorry for Joe, but now I kind of wish I was him.

Joe's sister shouts at us all to come into the kitchen and eat our dinner. The kitchen is small like ours, but we all fit inside. They all laugh and joke with each other. His sister even smiles at me, I try to smile back, I think I am smiling back but I'm not sure. I hope she doesn't think I'm strange. There is a big plate of chips in the middle of the table, we each have a plate with three sausages on. Joe grabs half the bowl of chips. His mum tuts and says she'll have to cook more now. No wonder he's so fat. His sister pours a drink into each of our glasses and tells me I can take more if I want it. I can feel myself go red.

"Tell Jay about when you went and stayed at your nan's house last year Joe."

"Why? It was boring. She don't have anything at her house. It smells like old people too."

"I thought you like going to stay at her house. She spoils you. You can go down to the beach every day. Have you ever been to the seaside Jay?

"No, mum's too busy to take me. I'd love to go though. I've never seen the sea."

"Why don't we take him with us next time we go?" It's his sister talking now, I know I've turned completely red. "I like him, he's not like that idiot, he doesn't say much. He could see the sea too."

"We'll see, he'd have to ask his mum and I'm not sure if your nan has enough room.

Now I'm excited. She wants me to go to the seaside with them. I hope they don't forget by the time the holiday comes. I hope mum will let me go. I remember she might not have any money. If she doesn't have any money I definitely won't be able to go. I'll try and think of a way I can make some money, but I'm just a little boy, I don't think I'll be able to do that. I'll do anything to be able to go with them. I don't feel so jealous anymore. I hope I find a way, if not I might have to take some money out of mum's drawer again. Just a little bit every now and again.

Everyone has finished their dinner except me. While they've been eating and talking, I've been dreaming of the seaside. Every time I look at his sister I turn away when she sees me, my face is probably really red by now, she still smiles though. Maybe she doesn't think I'm stupid. Joe gets up and pulls me by my sweater. We go into his room to play for a little while. His mum says I have to go in an hour or else my mum will get worried. I want to stay for longer but I don't want to tell her my mum won't be there when I get home so it doesn't matter.

Joe's room is filled with toys. He has pictures on the wall too. It's not like my room with just a bed and a small wardrobe. His is painted blue like I want to paint mine. There's carpet on the floor in here as well.

"How old is your sister?"

"14, she's an idiot though."

"She seems nice. I wish I had a sister"

"No, she isn't, she's an idiot. You can have her if you want."

"Will you really go to the seaside in the holidays?"

"Yeah, probably. We always do. I hope you can come, do you think you will? Will your mum let you?"

"I think so."

"Do you know when your dad is coming back yet? I can't wait to meet him. Don't tell anyone but I like singing too."

"Hahaha, you can't sing."

"Yes, I can! Next time we go to the woods I'll sing. I'm not doing it here because she'll come in and laugh at me. When's he coming back?"

"I'm not sure yet. Next year. If we're still friends then maybe he can tell his friends about you. When you grow up you can go and sing in Spain with him."

"What does he sing?"

"Songs"

"I know that, stupid. What kind of songs?"

"Just songs. Old ones. I don't really know them."

"Are you sure he's a singer?"

"Of course I am. I told you, when he comes next year you can meet him."

"Okay, but if you're lying to me, I'll never speak to you again. You can't come to the seaside with us either."

"I'm not lying. Just wait until next year."

"Okay."

"I better go now, my mum will wonder where I am."

"Oohh, can't you stay a little bit longer."

"Just for 10 minutes more."

"I'll show you my pictures before you go."

Joe walks over to a desk by the table. He opens the drawer and I can see lots of colouring pencils and pens. Pieces of paper too, all with lots of drawings on them. He shows me one of the pieces of paper. There's a drawing of a fat boy standing by a tree. There's a skinny boy standing on one of the branches.

"I drew it yesterday. That's you in the tree and that's me on the ground. I haven't really had many friends before, but I think you'll be a really good one. You can take it if you want."

My eyes feel as though they are about to pop. I don't want to cry. I take the picture from Joe's hand, I just smile, I can't speak because I know if I do I'll cry. I feel a bit silly. I've never really had any friends before. I know it's only been a week but Joe is the best friend I've ever had.

"He takes out another picture and it's of a man singing. I drew this one too, it's a singer. I don't know what your dad looks like but you can have it, it'll remind you of him."

37

I take the second picture and fold it up and put it in my pocket. I really wish I hadn't told him my dad was a singer. Joe's mum calls from outside his room. She says I have to go home now. I say goodbye to his mum and dad. His sister isn't there. I'm glad because I'm too shy to say goodbye to her. His mum gives me a packet of crisps to eat later. I don't really like crisps but I take them anyway. I say goodbye to Joe. As I'm walking out the door his mum shouts after me to not forget to ask my mum about the seaside.

Instead of walking straight home I take the long way back. All the way around the estate in a big circle. She'll not be back yet so it doesn't matter. As I'm walking I think about Joe and his family. I'd always thought what it would be like to have a big family. I'm not sure if I want one though, it's a bit noisy. I think Joe should be nicer to his sister, some people don't even have sisters even though they want one. They make plans too, like his dad wanting to take us to a football match and his mum talking about the seaside.

I take out the two pictures Joe gave me as I'm walking. I look at the picture of the singer. If I had a dad I wonder what he would be like. I wouldn't want him to be special, he doesn't need to be a singer. Even if he was like Joe's dad or the chip shop man. At least he would be there. We could talk about football, or he could take me out to the shops. Maybe he'd even take me to the seaside on the holidays. Mum wouldn't have to work so much if I had a dad. I look at the picture again and then looking away from it I scrunch it up into a ball and throw it onto the grass. I never cry but for the second time today I want to.

It's still bright so I walk back towards the woods and sit down by one of the trees, there is nobody around so I cry. My tears covering my face, dripping down on to the ground. I can taste the salt in my mouth. I think of singers, Joe's family, my mum and all the men that come to our house. I stand up and kick one of the tires that's lying on the floor. I kick it again and again, my tears coming faster. And then I stop. I sit down on the tyre I was just kicking. I use my t-shirt to wipe away my tears. I know my eyes will be still red. I just hope mum isn't there when I get home.

Opening the door I know she's at home. I can smell perfume and there is a pair of shoes by the door belonging to a stranger. I don't understand why they have to come so late. The evenings should be my time with my mum. I kick the shoes softly. Just touching them but it makes me feel better. I walk into the living room and sit down on the sofa. It's cold and there is no heating. The air is different in here, not like Joe's living room, It's warm in there. I don't know how but it just is. I hear laughter coming from mum's room. I decide to go to bed, I don't think I will see her tonight.

Lying on my bed I block out the sounds coming from the room next door. I try to think about what it will be like to go to the seaside with Joe and his family, then I remember I still don't know how I will get some money to go. More laughter, a deep voice, followed by a shushing sound. I cover my ears and hide under the blanket. I wonder what the sea sounds like. Tap, tap, tap, tap against the wall. Will there be any fish in the sea? Can I catch them? A loud bang, the sound of a slap and then a moan. I could buy ice cream and sit and watch the sea in the evening.

Her bedroom door slams shut followed by the front door. He's gone. I come out from underneath the blankets and turn on my small lamp that's by my bed. I wish I had some pictures up on the wall. Maybe I should draw some but I don't know how to. I could put up the pictures Joe gave me I don't have anything to stick it on the wall with. Then I remember there is some tape in the kitchen. I open the door quietly, not wanting her to hear me. I don't want to see her tonight. This is the first time I've not wanted to see her. I grab the tape that's sitting on top of the fridge and go back to my room. I hear a low moan coming from her room as I pass the door.

I close my bedroom door again and sit on my bed. I look around the room trying to decide where to put a picture. There's lots of places I can put it but I decide I'll put it opposite my bed so I can see it. I pick up my jeans and take Joe's picture of me and him and place it against the wall. I bite a piece of tape off and place it over the corner of the picture sticking it to the wall. Another three pieces and it's stuck nicely. I go back and sit on my bed and look at the picture and smile. I might not have a dad, and my mum is always busy, but at least I have a friend now.

I Hate That Woman

I know he goes in my room sometimes and takes a bit of money but it don't bother me, I wish I had some more I could give him. I don't like him eating all this junk food but he don't seem to be getting fat, maybe he ain't eating enough. I don't like him going in my room but I can't stop him if I ain't there, he's a good kid, he don't really cause me any trouble. He keeps wanting to tell me one of these stories he's made up but I haven't been around or I'm too tired when I come in to listen to it.

He reckons he's got a new friend that he met at school. That fat kid that belongs to her. If there's one person in my life that I wish would completely disappear it would be her. She always seems to be there, hanging around on that balcony, I can feel her eyes on me every time I leave the house. Stupid woman ain't got nothing better to do than to slag other people off to make her feel better about her own boring life. I don't really want him to go 'round there but I can't stop him having friends either, I'm happy he's got a little friend, just don't want her asking any questions.

I've decided I'm going to work from home now. It's too dangerous out there at night, there's been a few of the girls been attacked recently and one's gone missing. Don't know what happened to her, she might have overdosed in some crackhouse somewhere but no one has seen her. It ain't really that that bothers me though, if I'm home I'll be able to at least keep a better eye on him. I know I ain't the best mother in the world but I'm trying to do what's best for him. I hope it won't affect him too much.

I do wish he'd go out and play a bit more, not just standing outside the door kicking the ball against the wall. I know he's got this new friend but I wish he'd go and mix with some of the other kids. If he tried a bit harder to talk to them I'm sure they would let him hang around with them. It can't be healthy him in this house all the time, it must be why he has such a crazy imagination. I don't know how he thinks up half the stuff he does, some of his stories really do make me laugh, he could be a writer one day if he puts his mind to it.

I'd like to be able to get him out of here but I can't, I ain't got enough money. If we had a new start somewhere people don't know us I'm sure it would be a lot easier for him. I don't know how I'm going to be able to do it though. I ain't got any skills, they always said I was clever when I was at school but I really ain't sure about that. I ain't old but I reckon I'm too old to be going and learning new skills and getting a good job, besides, who is going to want to employ someone like me? I've never had a proper job in my life.

When I'd sing him to sleep as a baby I had these dreams of us moving away somewhere, maybe a little countryside town, or down by the seaside, living a nice quiet life, me with a little job so I can bring us in some money, him going to school and then to university, earning lots of money and us living happily ever after. That's how everyone thinks though ain't it? We all have these dreams but none of us ever seem to achieve them. All I worry about is how I'm going to have enough to put food on the table the next day.

I'm lonely too, I don't have anyone at all, none of my friends are real friends, they are just people I know. They ain't people I can really talk to, I've only ever had one person like that, Mrs Smith, but I'm getting more and more embarrassed to go and see her these days. That's what I really, really want. I want someone who I can tell everything too, tell them that I know I've made a complete fuck up of my life and I'm probably making a complete fuck up of the boy's life too but I don't know what to do, I don't know how to change it, I don't know how to control myself.

I don't know why I ever put them mirrors on the wall in my room, every time I sit on my bed all I can see is me looking back at myself. All I can think about is how much I hate myself, is there a word stronger than hate? If there is, that's how I feel when I look at myself in a mirror. I don't feel sorry for myself, I've made all the wrong decisions, it's me that's walked down that road I want to tell those kids in the park not to walk down. I had chances to stop and I never took them. I have a kid, a beautiful boy, an intelligent boy who could make something of himself, yet I still fuck it all up.

I do wonder sometimes if he would be better off without me, am I the one that's going to stop him making something of himself? Does he really need me in his life? I think about this every single day, guilt and anger that I'm not doing all I can to help him. It's destroying me and I don't know what I can do about it, I don't feel like there is anyone that will help me, all people do is judge me, just like that silly bitch standing on her balcony all day. I'd love her to live in my shoes just for one day so she would know what it's like, she wouldn't be so judgemental then.

Staying at Mrs Smith's

"You've got to stay at Mrs Smith's tonight, I've some friends coming round and it'll be too noisy for you."

"Okay". I don't mind going to Mrs Smith's, it's warmer there and she tells me about when she used to live in New Zealand. I sleep better there, I don't have to worry about whether mum will be home or not. I don't like her friends anyway, none of them are nice people, they're always shouting and drinking, it scares me a little bit. Last time she had friends round someone called the police because they were too loud, the policeman asked me if my mum treated me well, I told him she does.

"Mum..."

"What?"

"Can I go to the seaside with Joe on the holidays?"

"What? Just you and Joe?"

"No, his mum and dad and his sister, too. They asked me yesterday when I was at their house"

"What's their house like? I bet that miserable bitch didn't stop talking the whole time you was in there. What about his old man? I don't think I've ever seen him speak, no wonder with a wife like that."

"His mum was nice to me, his dad was too. Their house is quite nice, it's the same as this but they've got another room. They've got carpet on the floor too..."

"Well, when you're old enough, you can go out and get yourself a job and buy me some carpet, I ain't got the money to be putting carpets down."

"You've got money to have a party though…"

"Don't get cheeky with me, I work all the time, I'm entitled to have some fun."

"Sorry, just their house is nice and warm with carpets on the floor. Mum, what's a customer?"

"What? You know what a customer is, someone who goes in the shop and buys things."

"I know but Joe's mum said yesterday that you have customers…"

"You must have heard her wrong."

"What about the seaside? Can I go?"

"I'll have to see about it. I ain't promising you."

"Okay".

"Go to school, make sure you remember you've got to go to Mrs Smith's tonight, she'll have your dinner ready."

The estate looks a bit brighter this morning, maybe because I'm in a good mood, I know mum won't let me down, she'll find the money to let me go somehow. I don't really want to go to school today, they don't always pick on me, but you never know when, and I don't want them to ruin my good news. If I don't go, I don't know where I'll go. The only place I can think of is the small woods that me and Joe played in. If I go there it means I have to stay there all day, I don't know what I could do in there for a whole day, it is quiet though and no one will know I'm there. I take the small path that goes back behind the shops and into the wood, looking back at our door just in case mum is looking, she won't be, but just in case.

I find the place we played in last time and sit down next to the old washing machine. I wonder if when she has her parties mum thinks of me, does she tell her friends all about me? She must do, I'm her only son, she knows how much I love her, hopefully she tells them about how I did a good presentation at school, she might even tell them I have a new friend. If the police come this time at least I won't be there, no one around here likes them but the policeman that spoke to me seemed alright.

I think about the picture that Joe gave me. I wonder what it would be really like if I had a dad, if he was a singer too, and he lived in Spain. I would be able to go there every holiday and stay with him, he would have lots of money and mum wouldn't have to work. Nobody would call me names anymore, most of the kids would probably want to be my friend. I could go to a better school as well, one of them schools where you give money to go. Them things ain't important though, the most important thing is I would be able to have a dad.

I imagine what it would be like to have someone take me out to places, to speak to me when I'm sad, to tell me everything is okay. Most of the time I have to fight to hold back the tears, when I see the other kids having their mums outside when school finishes or sometimes I see the other kids playing football with their dads outside on the green, I know I won't ever have that. I wish I could have it for just one day, it doesn't have to be forever, even half a day, just so I know what it's like, so I know why all the other kids smile when they come out of the gates.

The woods are warm, I take my jacket off and put it down on top of the washing machine. I climb up the tree I climbed before, sitting there looking out at our estate, wondering what people are doing. I don't care that I haven't gone to school, they won't mind, they probably haven't even noticed. I know that school is good, when I grow up I don't want to live here anymore, I want to move somewhere else, somewhere where there's a beach, where it is hot all the time. I want to take mum with me, I can make lots of money and she can be happy, she won't have to work.

I lie back against the washing machine and dream of being grown up. I want to be a writer, sell all my stories to people all over the world so they can read them, people will know my name, I won't just be that kid with no dad and the mum that nobody likes. They'll all want to be friends with me then. I'll buy a big house, Joe can come over, he can draw pictures in my books so he can make some money. We can both remember the times that the other kids made fun of us and laugh about them while they are all still here and we are both rich and famous!

I hear something rustling in the bushes and a man comes out and falls over, he had a can in his hand but he's dropped and the beer has spilled all over the ground. I don't think he has noticed me, I think he's talking to himself. I don't know whether to get up and run or stay and see if he goes away. He just lies there, his clothes are all old and dirty, there are stains on his trousers, his beard is all yellow and white. He moves his head looking towards me and then closes his eyes. I get up and run, running all the way to school. When I get there I tell the receptionist I had to go to the dentist, she says next time I need to bring a letter.

Nobody takes any notice of me as I walk into the classroom almost two hours late. They all have their heads down. Joe looks up at me and smiles, I smile back at him, I can't wait to tell him about what I just saw. I sit down in an empty space, the girl I've sat next to me looks at me funny and moves her chair further away, looking at her friend and then giggling. She starts drawing something on a piece of paper and then shows it to her friend and they both look at me and start laughing. I look away from them as the teacher tells them to be quiet, what have I done to any of these kids?

I keep looking up at the clock hoping lunch time will come quicker but it is taking longer. Every time I look only a minute has passed. Finally the bell rings and I can get away from them. As I'm walking out the door the teacher calls me back.

"Why were you late this morning?"

"I had to go to the dentist."

"You didn't tell me that before today, you know you're supposed to, I need you to get a letter from your mum to explain why you were late."

"Okay, but not tomorrow, she won't be home tonight."

"Is everything okay at home?"

"Yes."

"If you ever have any problems you can talk to me, you seem very quiet recently"

"Miss, if I want to be a writer what do I have to do?"

"Anyone can be a writer, but I think you need to be good at school and then go to university, I think you can do that."

"Okay Miss, thank you."

"Remember what I said, if you have any problems come and see me, I'm not going to tell anyone."

I walk away without answering, I don't know what kind of problems she's talking about. At least she thinks I can be a writer though. I feel better now she's said that, I go to get my dinner and sit down next to Joe who is sitting on his own away from everyone else. He looks like he's been crying but I'm not sure, sometimes his face gets red because he runs to fast to the dinner line.

"Where did you go this morning?"

"I went to the woods. Something happened but I can't tell you."

"Why not? Why did you go to the woods? Did you go on your own?"

"Yeah, it's a secret, I'm not sure you will keep a secret."

"I can! I didn't even tell anyone about your dad yet!"

"Shhhhh! I'll tell you later on the way home."

"Why can't you tell me now!"

"I'll tell you later!"

He frowns as he finishes his dinner and then gets up and walks away. Now he really wants to know what happened, I'm going to have to make the story a bit more exciting. An old man falling down in front of me isn't really that interesting.

When school is over I wait for Joe outside the gates. I watch as the other kids meet their parents and tell them about their day at school. They walk off happily talking to each other, the two girls that were laughing at me earlier skipping away, not even noticing me as I pass. Joe walks out through the gates, his face red as usual, struggling to catch his breath. We set off towards home, the school now quiet, everyone else has gone home.

"What happened then? I had to wait behind, Miss wanted to ask me something."

"You won't tell anyone?"

"I told you I won't!"

"This morning I didn't go to school because I didn't want to. I went to the woods instead." His eyes looking at me as though I'm crazy.

"If I didn't go to school, my mum really would kill me."

"I was near where we were last time, sitting by the old washing machine and my dad came and found me."

"I thought he was in Spain? How did he know you were in the woods?"

"He followed me from when I left home. He could only stay for an hour because he had to go back to Spain, he said next year you can come to Spain with me and we can visit him."

"Really?", I don't think he believes me.

"I told him you like drawing and singing too, he said you'd love it over there." His eyes light up a little bit.

"I don't think my mum would let me go, I can ask though!"

"Don't ask her just yet, wait until next year when I'm sure we can go."

"Okay" he says with a confused look on his face.

We walk the rest of the way in silence, I'm kicking a stone, hoping he believes me. He looks like he's thinking.

"I like you because you're my friend you know, not because your dad's a singer. You don't have to tell lies."

"I'm not telling lies, you'll see next year when we go together! I have to go this way now anyway, I'm not staying at home tonight, my mum is having a party."

"You staying with that old lady?"

"How do you know that?"

"Nothin', my mum said sometimes you stay with the old lady."

"Yeah, I am. I'll meet you in the morning if you like, wait for me opposite my house."

"Okay, don't be late though, my mum can see your house from our balcony, she'll get angry if she sees me waiting around."

Mrs Smith's house is clean, she has lots of them things you use to measure the temperature on her walls, she says she collects them, every new place she goes to she buys one. She must have been to a lot of places. Some of them have the name of a place or country written on them but most of them I have never heard of before. Her sofa is really comfortable too, I sit there waiting as she goes off into the kitchen to make me a sandwich and some orange juice. Her book case is full of books, sometimes I sit there for hours looking through them, especially the ones with lots of pictures in them, I like the one about animals in Africa the most.

She comes back in with my food and drink and puts it down on the coffee table.

"How has school been? I haven't seen you much recently."

"It's okay, a little bit boring, sometimes I don't want to go."

"You know you have to. How's your mother?"

"She's okay, she's busy a lot though, I don't see her much, she's at home but there are people there with her. She looks tired all the time."

"You can come here whenever you want, you know that. I've got some new books you might like, there's a new atlas there, it's got pictures of places around the world."

"Mrs Smith?"

"Yes…"

"What does my mum do?"

"She's a nurse, love. You know that."

"There are scratches on her arm but I don't know how she got them. I'm too scared to ask in case she gets angry."

"She probably just hurt herself doing something. I wouldn't worry about it, love. I've known your mum since she was your age, she loves you and she's only trying to do her best."

"I know, I just wish I saw her more."

Her eyes look a bit watery.

"Things will get better, just make sure you keep going to school, don't worry about your mum too much, if you have any problems come and see me."

"Okay. I'll read some books for a little while if that's okay?"

"Of course it is love, you can take them up to your room if you like, I'll call you when dinner is ready."

"Okay, thank you."

I just take the atlas upstairs with me. I love looking at the different countries of the world but this book has pictures too. I imagine myself in all these places, walking in Africa with elephants while the sun is setting, in Japan climbing that mountain with the snow on the top. I know one day I'm going to go to these places. I'm going to try my hardest to do the best for me and mum. I don't care what anyone else here thinks about us. I feel warm thinking about getting away.

Mrs Smith wakes me from my day dreams as she calls me for dinner. We sit together in silence, she is the only person I like sitting with and saying nothing. When we are finished we sit down in the living room together.

"What was my dad like?"

"He was a good man, when he met your mother he was too young."

"Why did he go?"

"He was too young, love. It wasn't because of you, he just didn't know how to look after you and your mum so one day he left. No one knows where he went, he wasn't from around here."

"Where do you think he went?"

"No idea, he was from the other side of London, maybe he went back there, your mum tried to find him but she couldn't, his mother wouldn't tell her where he was."

"Do you think he'll ever come and find me?"

"He might do, I wouldn't hold out too much hope though, you might be disappointed."

"It hurts me when they make fun of me for not having a dad."

"I know, love, but kids are cruel. Not all of them have dads either, I know most of their mothers, your mum is no angel but neither are theirs, take no notice of them."

"I didn't go to school yesterday…"

"Why not?"

"I didn't want to, it's too boring."

"I told you earlier, you have to go to school. Where did you go?"

"I went into the woods for a couple of hours and a man came along and fell over so I ran away and went to school."

"I told you not to go in there, look if you don't want to go to school, you come here, don't go wandering the streets on your own. Don't do it often though or I'll tell your mother."

"Okay"

"Don't tell your mother I said anything about your father either, she'll be annoyed. Now go to bed and read for a bit. I'll wake you up in the morning."

I go upstairs to the bedroom, I can see down to where our house is, there are people standing around outside the door, I'm not sure what they're doing. I can make out mum, her high heels and red skirt, I can see she's laughing and joking. I get underneath the covers of the bed without taking my clothes off, I just want to hide away.

Dreaming of Snowmen

There's a big house in front of me, it's cold outside, there's snow on the floor, in the garden of the house is a big snowman. His nose is a carrot, he has big, round, black eyes, they look like happy eyes. His mouth is made of stones, a wide smile. From the window there is a glow of warmth, there doesn't seem to be anyone inside. I walk up to one of the large windows and look inside, there's a big fire burning, a black cat lying on its back in front of it. The room has decorations, a massive Christmas tree in the corner, colourful, the lights twinkling.

I walk to the door, it's open, I push the door open and walk inside. I can feel the warmth straight away. Something is pulling me to the room I saw through the window. The cat rolls over as I walk in, purring loudly. I walk over to the tree, touching the branches, it's real, I've never touched a real one before. There are boxes and boxes of presents underneath it, like you see on the television or in the windows of those big shops on Oxford Street. There are names written on little tags but I can't read them, it's just a blur.

I look up, the ceiling is so tall, whoever lives here must be rich. I walk over to the fireplace, there are photographs resting against the wall. Like the words, I can't make out who are in the pictures, there are people but it's all so blurry, I wonder who they are? I think there is a boy, a woman and a man, all standing together, I move closer trying to see who they are but they become more blurred, now I can't even make out the outlines of the people. I step back from the fireplace, the cat looks up at me and meows, stands up quickly and then runs out of the room.

My feet are warm, I look down and see I have no shoes on. Why weren't they cold when I was outside? There's a rug beneath them, it's so soft on my feet. I sit down on it, feeling the heat of the fire on my body, I don't want to get up again, I wish I could stay here forever. I look back over at the tree, presents everywhere, even some on the branches, I'm sure they weren't there before. The little boy or girl that lives here must be really lucky. I wonder where the cat went to? I've always wanted a cat, maybe I should go and see.

Back out in the large hallway I see there are stairs going up to another floor. Did the cat go up? I should look anyway. I'm in a stranger's house but I don't feel scared, I don't feel like I shouldn't be here. At the top of the stairs there are so many doors, I open the one in front of me. The room is painted blue and there are pictures and posters all over the wall. There's a large bed next to another big window. The bed looks so comfortable, the floor is covered with carpet. I walk to the bed and sit on the end of it, looking out the window I see so many tall buildings and bright lights, it looks like the city but I'm not sure.

There is snow falling, it looks like one of them toys that you can buy. The ones you shake and the snow covers a city or a snowman or a house. I always wanted one of them. Most of the buildings are just long dark shapes with lights shining out, I don't recognise them, except for one. I can see it clearly through the dark of the night and the thick snow that's falling. There's only one light on in that building, it's coming from the bottom floor. I can even see the shape of a small boy sitting down outside of the window the light is coming from. It's so clear, but it's so far away, how can I see it? He gets up, kicks a stone and walks away and then it all becomes blurred and far away, I can only see the light.

I look up at all the posters on the wall, some of them are pictures somebody has drawn themselves. There's a boy holding hands with another boy, one of them is really fat. There are posters of someone singing but I don't recognise the man. Most of the posters are of the singer. I stand up and look closer but I still don't recognise him. These people are rich, maybe it's a singer I've never heard of before, like classical music or something. I walk over to a big desk that is in one corner of the room. There's paper and pens spread all over it. I reach to pick a piece of paper up but I can't, my fingers seem to go right through it. The words written on it are like the labels on the presents, blurred, I can't read them.

Suddenly I hear voices, I should be scared but I'm not, I'm in someone else's house but I feel like I know the house even though I've never been here before. I think I know the voices too. I walk back out of the room and down the stairs, the voices are coming from the room with the fireplace and Christmas tree inside. I push the door open, the room is full of people, none of them turn to look at me except for one, a lady, I know her but she looks different, it's my mum. Her face doesn't look the same, her cheeks are red and she is smiling, her eyes look bright, she walks over to me and picks me up and then walks back to the chair she was sitting on with me in her arms.

Sitting next to her is the man I just saw on the posters, I know it's him. Why could I see his face but the other pictures were all blurred? He has dark hair, he is tall, even though he is sitting down I know he's tall. Mum rests her hand on his leg, he squeezes her hand. They are talking to people but I don't know who any of them are. I can't really see their faces properly, it's only mum and the man whose faces are clear. Mum's clothes are new, they look expensive too. I don't know what she is saying to the other people, it's just a noise, not a bad noise, I like it, it's soft, it make me want to go to sleep.

She lifts me up again and carries me over to the tree, she puts me down in front of all the presents, smiles and walks back to sit next to the man. The man looks at me, smiles and waves, I smile back but I still don't know who he is. Mum points at the presents and then carries on talking to the faceless people. I take one of the presents, it's a big box with a ribbon and a bow on top of it, I feel like I shouldn't open it, I look towards mum and she meets my eyes and smiles, she's telling me to open it. I pull at the bow but it doesn't come off, I try to pull the ribbon away but it won't move. Now I can't even lift the box, it just won't move.

I try to move another present but it's stuck to the floor too, I can't take off any of the ribbons. I look back at mum and she just smiles and carries on talking. All of these presents in front of me and I can't open any of them. I wonder what is inside them? I look up at the tree and see there are sweets hanging from the branches. Red and white, shaped like a walking stick, I try to take one but I can't, my hand just goes through it, I reach again and the same thing happens. I kick out at the presents but nothing happens, as my foot is about to hit it, it slows down and just taps them.

Mum comes back over and takes me by the hand, we walk back to the chairs and sit down. The man stands up and walks to the fireplace, he turns around and starts to sing, I think he is singing but there isn't any noise coming from his mouth. I look up at mum, I've never seen her smile like this before. Her cheeks are so red, her skin isn't pale, she doesn't look like she is sick. The man walks out of the room and mum takes me by the hand again, walking me back up the stairs and into the room with the blue walls. The cat is asleep on the bed, mum lifts me up and puts me into the bed, she sits down on the floor next to it and starts to talk, I don't know what she is saying but I like the sound.

The man appears at the door, he walks up to the bed and sits down next to mum. He reaches out and ruffles my hair and listens to mum. She's smiling as she's talking, the man gets up again and waves at me, smiling and happy. Mum gets up and follows him out the door, she looks back as she leaves and then walks out shutting the door. The room is completely dark, I can't see the blue walls or the posters. There are no curtains on the windows, I look out and can see that dark block again, I can see the boy sitting on his own. Now I'm next to him, I don't think he can see me. He keeps looking up at the red door behind us. It looks like home, the door opens and a man walks out and away from the house, the little boy gets up, head still down and walks into the house. I'm cold again, I don't want to be here I want to go back to that other house.

Mrs Smith

I've lived around here for nearly thirty years, I've seen people come and go, I know most of the families that live here. Well I don't know them but I know what they get up to. It's changed a lot since back then but I still like it, it ain't as bad as some people say it is but I still don't really like going out at night. Most of them wouldn't do anything to anyone living on the same estate, you can't be too careful though. There are a few shady characters, but they don't seem to bother anyone, they just get up to whatever it is they get up to.

I come back here after I lived in New Zealand. I got married too young and went there with my husband. After being there for ten years I decided to come back. Left him behind without even saying anything, he never tried to contact me either. It was boring there and I missed home. I still like to travel though, I try to get away once a year and see somewhere new. A lot of them around here don't understand that, they live in a bubble, there ain't nothing out there that they think they want. That's why I tell young Jay he needs to go to school and get away.

I knew her mum when she was a kid. Her mum and me used to go to the pub on Friday nights together, it's gone now that pub, sometimes I wish it was still around, it was a good place to meet people and have a chat. She was a good girl back then, never got into trouble, used to go to school all the time, she wanted to be a nurse. Her mum always used to talk about her when we were together, she had high hopes for her. It's a shame really, I don't know, sometimes things happen in life that lead you down the wrong path. I just hope she doesn't take the kid down it too.

Her mum used to do cleaning jobs and if she was late she'd come around mine and I'd give her some tea. I never had children with my husband, he couldn't have kids but he never told me until we got to New Zealand. I suppose that's why I used to like looking after her, I like looking after the boy as well. They're so full of ideas kids, I love their imaginations. She used to tell me about all the places she wanted to go when she grew up, how she wanted to leave the estate and go and live abroad. She loved to tell stories too, a lot like the boy.

As she grew up something changed in her, it was like she lost her love for life. I don't even know why, it might have been her dad leaving but she stopped coming around as often, when she did she didn't really say much, it was like she was just coming around because she felt she had to. I knew she was hanging around with the wrong people but I didn't say anything, I'm sure her mum knew anyway but she didn't say nothing either. It used to make me sad seeing the young girl with a bright face and bright ideas become so distant. She'd still borrow books off me though, it was like she was still clinging on to escaping.

I probably should have done more to help her, but I didn't know what was wrong. I thought she'd just grow out of it. When I was out of an evening and I saw her out and about she'd pretend she didn't see me. I wouldn't say anything to her mum because I didn't want her to think I was interfering. In a way I kind of blame myself for the way she turned out, I knew her mum was innocent and wouldn't be able to see something was wrong with her. I did try one night we was at the pub together but she wouldn't listen.

She stopped coming altogether for a couple of years. That was when she left school. Her mum said she had a new boyfriend and that he was nice. Then she ended up getting pregnant and her mum stopped coming out. I don't know if she was embarrassed or what but I hardly ever saw her after that until she died a year later, not long after the boy was born. The boyfriend moved into the flat and I saw them out together, she'd stop and talk to me but didn't really say much, it was like we'd lost a connection. I did hear her mum hit the bottle when the old man left but I don't know how true that was.

After she had the kid and her mother died everything went wrong for her. The fella left, just walked out one day. No one knew where he went and the mother wouldn't tell her either. She'd had a kid, her mother had died and now the boyfriend had just up and left. She turned up at my door one day in tears holding the baby, he wouldn't stop crying and she didn't know what to do. She was completely broken, I've never seen anyone in as much of a mess as she was that day. I said I'd look after the boy a couple of times a week for her.

After that she'd come around quite often, it was like she'd found a bit of strength from somewhere. She said when he was a bit older she was going to find a job and look after him properly, make sure he could do all the things she had missed out on doing. She missed the father, even though he'd run away she wouldn't say a bad word about him. She was struggling though, I could see that, too much had happened at once and she didn't know how to cope, she said she was coping, but I knew she wasn't.

As the boy got older I would still look after him. He's a good kid, like his mum when she was his age. He loves his books and he loves to tell his stories. I can't help but think he's a bit innocent though, he seems clever in some ways but in others I don't know if he just ignores it all or just doesn't know what it is going on. It was when he was about 3 that I knew she was on drugs, she told me herself. She said she needed it, it helped her cope. I don't know nothing about drugs but I knew it won't help when you're bringing up a kid.

One of the other girls that lives down near them told me she'd seen men coming and going at all hours of the night. Everyone knows what's going on but the kid. Thing is I've never spoken to her about it. I know she knows it isn't right and I know she knows everyone talks about her but I want her to be able to have someone she can come and talk to and keep her company. She hasn't got any friends, not real ones anyway, they're all just people that use her. It's like she craves their attention. I don't know, maybe one day she'll just stop and realise.

When you see a little girl that was the way she was grow up and change so much to how she is now, it's hard. I can't really do anything about it, she ain't going to listen to me, I just want to try and help the boy as much as I can. Things have been getting a bit out of hand recently though, I think he might be finally realising that something isn't right, he keeps asking questions, I just try to give him an answer he wants to hear. At least if I help him it might make me feel a bit less guilty about not being able to help her. My biggest worry is she'll end up dead.

Can I Go to the Seaside?

There are only a couple of weeks left until the summer holiday. Mum still hasn't said whether I'm able to go to the beach or not. I keep asking her but she says she will think about it and then doesn't say anything. She seems even more tired lately, there are more scratches on her arms, she hardly speaks to me when I come home from school. I'm not sure what I can do, I told Mrs Smith but she said she doesn't know what's wrong with her. I thought about telling my teacher but Mrs Smith said if I did that they might take me away to live somewhere else.

Next year is my last year at primary school, when I go to a new school I might be able to make some more friends, the kids at the new school won't all know me. I hope Joe will go to my school too, but I'm not sure, he says his mum wants him to go to a school far away, she reckons the school near us is rubbish. He hasn't asked me about my dad recently, I'm glad he hasn't because I don't really like lying. Since I told him about the time I was in the wood I don't see him that much but he said he still wants me to come to the beach with them.

I went to the shop last week to buy some cigarettes for mum and I saw his sister, she smiled at me and waved. I waved back, the other kids that were with her laughed but she didn't, at least she seems kind. The ones she hangs around with are the ones I see in the park at night drinking, I hope she doesn't get into any trouble with them. Her mum will go down there and start fighting with them probably. I saw his mum the other week, she asked me why I don't come round, I just told her I've been busy.

The door to the flat is slightly open to the flat, usually when I get home mum is in the kitchen but there isn't anyone there today. I open the fridge and take out a coke I bought when I went to get her cigarettes. I sit down on the table and drink it slowly, trying to think of how I can ask her if I can go to the beach or not. I sit there for half an hour, wondering where she has gone and if she is going to come back tonight. I had better check her room to see if she might be inside sleeping, I'm hungry and want something to eat.

Opening the door I see mum lying across the bed, there are little bits of red on the white rug that is next to her bed. I'm scared, she isn't moving and I don't know what to do. I quickly walk over to the bed and try and turn her over, as I push her on to her back she lets out a moan. There is a cut above her eye, it's still bleeding a little bit. As I push her over something falls on the floor from the bed. I look down at the floor, it's a needle like I see sometimes in the park. I leave it on the floor, go out to the kitchen and pour a glass of water and throw it on her face.

Her eyes open slightly, a smile appears on her face. She reaches out her hand and takes mine and softly squeezes it.

"Mum? Are you okay? What's the matter?"

"I'm okay, I'm just resting. Go and get yourself some dinner."

"Your eye looks hurt. You need to get a plaster for it."

"It's fine, just go and get some money from my purse and get yourself something to eat from the chip shop."

Her eyes are barely open and I'm still scared. She can talk though so she must be okay. I don't know what to do. Maybe I should go and get Mrs Smith, she will know what to do. I'm worried if I go and get her mum might be angry. If I call the police or an ambulance she might be even more angry. What if they come and take me away? There's still a smile on her face but she has let go of my hand. I put my hand on her forehead and stroke her hair back across her head. There are tears coming again. I curl up into a ball next to her holding her hands into my chest, if I go to sleep maybe when I wake up everything will be okay.

I wake up a little while later, I'm not sure how long I've been asleep but she has rolled away from me and seems to be sleeping. I put my hand on her chest to make sure she is breathing, I take it away and then put it back again, just to make sure. I sit up on the side of the bed with my feet on the floor. As I look down I can see the needle, I had forgotten about it. I pick it up and look at it, I've only ever seen them in the park or when the nurse comes to school. She must be using them for her patients. I drop it back on the floor.

I take one more look at her to make sure she is alive, I can see her breathing and feel more relaxed. I take one of the tissues that are in the box by her bed and wipe my eyes and nose. I take her purse out of her bag and find some money to get some food. I forget that I haven't looked at the time yet, there might not be anywhere open. I take her hand and look at her watch, still only nine o clock, the chip shop will still be open. One last time I check if she is breathing and leave the room and straight out the door.

I see that there is a black car outside, the window is down and the man that was in our house before is inside it. He sees me.

"Where's your mum?"

"I don't know."

"You sure she ain't inside?"

"Nah, she wasn't in when I got back from school. I haven't seen her today."

"You better not be lying to me..."

"I ain't, she ain't inside, I don't know where she's gone."

"Tell her when you see her I'm looking for her and I want my money. Remember to tell her 'money'."

"What money?"

"Don't worry about that, it ain't got nothing to do with you, all I want you to do is tell her I want my money, she's probably fucked up on skag somewhere, I feel sorry for you kid. Your mother needs to sort herself out, she shouldn't be treating children like that."

He smiles as he says this, a nasty smile I don't like, it makes me feel scared. He drives off and I feel relieved. I'm not sure what he is talking about though. I make my way towards the chip shop thinking about what to do with mum. She doesn't seem to be dying and she was breathing, maybe I should just leave her there. I don't think I will go to school tomorrow, I will just go to Mrs Smith's, it will be the first time since that day I went to the woods that I haven't been to school, Mrs Smith won't mind. I think I'll have to stay up all night and watch mum.

When I reach the chip shop he looks as though he is about to close but when he sees me he lets me in the door.

"Hurry up, I'm busy, tonight I close early but for you I do you a favour. Tell me what you want and I make it quickly."

"Chips and a sausage, and a coke too please."

"You have good manners, boy."

I smile back at him but I don't want to talk. For once he doesn't seem too bothered, he has his own troubles. He fries a sausage for me and even does a fresh batch of chips. When I go to give him the money he says "Why you so quiet?"

"I'm not, I'm just a bit tired."

"You go home and go to bed, you shouldn't be walking around here so late, it's dangerous, them kids will take your money if they see you."

"I'm okay, they won't do anything. See you later."

I look up at his clock as I'm leaving and see I've only been gone for 20 minutes. There's nobody around as I walk home, not even any kids. As I approach the door I can see that it isn't shut properly. I feel scared again, what if I didn't shut it and that man has come back and found mum. I walk quickly and then slowly again, I don't want to see him, if he knows I lied I don't know what he will do to me. I push the door quietly, mum's shoes have gone. I rush into her room and she's not there. The needle isn't on the floor anymore.

I put the sausage and chips on the kitchen table and sit down. I'm not hungry, I only bought it because I should eat. I don't know why but I pick up the food and throw it against the wall, I get up and kick it where it has fallen on the floor, I kick it all over the kitchen. I don't even know why I'm angry, I just am. I pick my keys back up again and walk back out the door. I don't know where I'm going, I just keep walking away from the estate. It's dark and there aren't many people on the roads. An old man walking his dog passes me and looks at me in surprise, I just keep walking.

I walk towards the park that's behind our school. There is a hill there and I climb up to the top of it. I can see across the city, all the lights from the buildings in the night sky. I can see our block too, I wonder what the other kids are doing, probably sitting with their families watching tele or maybe they are even in bed after their mums have called them in for the night and cooked them dinner. I don't know where my mum has gone. I don't know what happened to her earlier, why was her face hurt?

I think about Mrs Smith's atlas and all the different countries and pictures that are inside it. I wish I was in one of them places now. I don't want to be here, I want to run away, I'm angry at my mum, I've never been angry at her before, I'm not even sure why I'm angry at her. That man outside frightened me too. Why can't she tell me where my dad is? Why can't she get a job that doesn't mean lots of people come to our house? Maybe I should go and look for my dad myself but I don't even know what his name is.

It's not cold outside and the grass is dry. I lie back and look up at the sky. Black with little stars everywhere. Places so far away. I close my eyes and go back to my forest. The forest where all the animals live and protect me from bad people. I'm walking among the big trees and there is an elephant washing himself in a river. He moves his trunk, calling me over to him. I jump into the river with him and he splashes me with water. I climb onto his back and he carries me off into the jungle. As we pass the trees other animals appear, like they are pleased to see me.

We stop and the elephant lets me down onto the floor of the forest, he walks away and leaves me. There are monkeys above my head looking down at me, it looks like they are pointing at me and laughing, screaming and shouting. I look over my hands and body and realise all my clothes are old and torn. My shoes have fallen off, I want to run away now, I feel like they don't want me here anymore. From the bushes a man appears and walks towards me. I don't know who he is, he takes my hand and tells me to come with him, he will take me somewhere safe. The sounds of the monkeys fading away as we walk, I feel safe, I'm not scared anymore.

I wake up suddenly, not sure where I am. It's completely dark as I sit up and seeing all the buildings in the distance I remember where I am. I put my head in my hands and cry again. I never used to cry but now I want to cry all the time. I'm scared, I don't want to go home, I don't know who will be there, I don't know if mum will have come home yet, maybe that man will be there again, I don't want to see him, what if mum is lying on the bed again and I can't wake her up. I don't know what to do and I don't know who to ask.

73

I get up and walk back towards the estate. This time there are no people on the street, it must be really late, most of the lights in the buildings have been turned off. It feels strange being out on the streets on my own at night, I actually like it, I feel free when there is nobody about. Turning onto the estate I see the same black car that was outside earlier that the man had been in. I'm scared again, I walk towards the chip shop and peer in through the window to see what time it is on the clock, it says it's 3 am. I must have slept outside for a long time.

I don't want to go back inside the house, not if that man is there, mum might not even know I haven't gone out, she doesn't check to see if I'm in my room when she comes back these days. I don't have anywhere to go though, I'm supposed to go to school at eight, I will have to come back by then. I walk off back towards the woods and the bit where the washing machine is. I see my jacket it is still there, nobody has taken it. I lay it on the floor and then lie down on top of it and try to sleep. I keep hearing noises that make me jump, so I sit up and lean against the washing machine, waiting until I think it's time to go back.

The sun has been up for an hour I think, it should be okay to go back by now. I walk back to the house and the car has gone. I open the door quietly hoping she won't hear me. I go into my room, change my clothes and then make some noise slamming the bedroom door. There doesn't seem to be anyone here. I open the door to mum's room, it's empty but it looks tidier than it did yesterday. There is some money on the side of her bed, only a pound altogether but I take it. There is another shiny piece of paper next to the lamp on the bedside table, there are brown marks on it.

I go into the kitchen and the food I left on the floor yesterday has all been cleaned up. I take some milk out of the fridge and drink a glass. I have to remember to buy some on my way home after school. As I sit down to finish another glass I see there is a piece of paper with something written on it. It is in mum's handwriting.

Sorry about last night, mum was really tired, thank you for coming in to see if I was okay. I left some money on the table next to my bed for you, you can get some dinner with it tonight because I won't be home. Why was your dinner all over the floor when I came in last night? I had to clean it all up. I hope you ate some of it and went to bed early. You're going to have to go and stay at Mrs Smith's house for a few days soon, I'm going to be really busy. I'm really sorry. You have to tell your friend you can't go to the beach with him, I don't have any money to let you go. Next year I will take you. Don't tell anyone about yesterday. Mum x

If I tell someone will they take me away? I think I want to be taken away. I can't go to the seaside with Joe and his family, I never see my mum and now I have to go and stay in someone else's house because she is too busy. I take the piece of paper and turn the cooker on, I put the corner to where the fire is and let it burn, it falls to the ground on fire and I panic, jumping on it to make it go out. If she ain't going to be home today I'm just going to stay here, nobody will know.

I go back in to her room and look through her wardrobe, I find a jumper she used to wear when I was only three. I hold it up to my nose and smell it. I wish it was them times again, she was always here then, she never let me out of her sight. I climb under the covers of her bed still clutching the jumper tight to my face, tears streaming down my face onto the jumper. I fall asleep again, sleep is the only place I can run to away to, but even that isn't very nice, I hope I won't go back to the forest, I just want to go somewhere I have a mum and a dad.

Don't End Up Like Me

I had always wanted to keep him separate from it all, I don't want him to see or to know, I don't know why I thought I'd be able to get away with it. That he has just seen me the way I was lying on the bed is breaking my heart. What must he think of me? A young child who only wants the best for his mum and he probably thought I was dead. I didn't even have it in me to face him when I sent him out. I'm dealing with it the only way I know, it's the wrong way to deal with it but I don't know what else I can do.

Sitting here in this room, on an old and battered sofa, the wallpaper is coming off the walls, there is rubbish all over the floor, bodies spread out across the room, no one caring if they are dead or alive, that's not what is important. What is important is getting what you need to hide away from the rest of the world. If they're dead, there's even a bit of envy, you want to be like they are, free from all pain, free from all the things that you are tied to. I've run away again, and this is the place that I've run away from, a room full of despair and misery.

There's a kid sitting on the floor opposite me. She's sitting underneath a window and there is a small crack in the curtain that allows a beam of light to shine just over her head. She looks angelic, her face isn't yet thin and worn, her skin not stretching over her cheekbones, she's on something but her eyes aren't dead yet, they will be soon, give it a few months and she'll look no different to anyone else in here, but at the moment she is a glimpse back into the past for everyone in the room. You never ask what people are running from, it'll only be a tale far more miserable than your own.

I stand up to leave, catching my balance as I reach my feet. Opening the door the light blinds me, I'm numb, there is no feeling, even simple things like the sun don't bring joy to me anymore. Walking down the stairs I pass an old couple who move to the side as I pass them, their eyes looking at the floor, scared, not wanting any trouble. It's small, but there is a feeling of guilt, guilt that people are scared to walk up and down the stairs in the place where they live. Or is it guilt for not staying at home and looking after my boy? I don't know, I don't know why I feel anything.

The estate I'm on is half an hour away from my own. I don't know anybody here, but I do remember coming here as a kid because there was a small park that had a swing that I liked. I'd sit on the swing for hours while my mum would push me, when she got tired I would just sit in it, trying to push myself but not really knowing how to. The park is still there, it doesn't seem to have changed, the swing looks the same, even the seat my mum used to sit and watch me from doesn't look like it has been replaced.

I sit down on it, still able to fit. If there's one thing good about being on drugs it's that I lose weight. I swing back and forwards and close my eyes, imagining mum is sitting on the bench opposite watching me, telling me to be careful and not to swing too high, I can see the smile on her face even though she wants to pretend to be concerned. I can hear her voice, it's comforting. I open my eyes again, there's no one sitting on the seat, the sun has disappeared behind the clouds and a small breeze is blowing.

I get off the swing and walk over to the bench she used to sit on. Looking over at the swing I realise I haven't taken him to the park for years, I have never watched him on the swing, I've never taken him away anywhere. He lives my pain and misery not through choice but because he has to, I know I have a choice and me not making a choice means there is no better way for him until I do make the right one. I just don't know how I'm going to be able to do it, I still feel like that kid sitting in the swing, but I'm scared and frightened, not happy and free with someone watching over me.

He probably thinks I'm not going to let him go to the beach because I don't love him, but I do, he's the only thing that keeps me from ending it all. It's my own selfishness that won't let him go, I don't want him to see what kind of life he could have if he had normal parents, what kind of life he could have if his mum wasn't fucked up on drugs all the time. If he sees that, he'll never want to come back to me, I don't want him taken away from me. They'll show him the life I wanted to give him but don't know how to give.

I can see him now, sat in his room alone, wondering where I went, how I managed to get myself in the state that I got myself into this morning. He'll know he can't go away with his little friend, he's probably angry. I'm angry too, angry at myself, I hate myself, not just hate, I despise myself for putting him through all this. I don't think anyone understands that, they just see the junkie mum who doesn't care about her kid, they don't know how I feel, how much I wish I could start again, they only judge me, they never put out a hand to help.

I'm Not a Kid Anymore

Funny ain't it? People that used to be your friend and now they won't even acknowledge you. Joe's just walked past me, didn't even say a word. I used to stick up for that kid. I've even still got that picture he drew for me in my drawer. I don't want it on my wall anymore, a 15 year old with a drawing on his wall of some kid that's supposed to be his friend is a bit wrong. Not that anyone would see it, I don't have anyone that would come round my house. I don't think Joe ever even saw it on the wall.

We didn't even fall out. We just kind of stop speaking to each other, when he came back from the seaside he started losing weight and the other kids didn't tease him anymore, he made other friends. Someone said his mum put a brick through the window of the chip shop. I never asked the man that owns it but it wouldn't surprise me. She did it before with that other shop. He's quite popular now, I'm just the same as I always was, no real friends. He don't tease me or anything, he just doesn't talk to me.

When I couldn't go to the beach, that was when it started. When he asked me why I couldn't go I told him that my dad was taking me to New Zealand. I don't think he believed me, looking back I wouldn't believe me either, it was a stupid thing to say. Still it got me a friend for a while. Maybe he asked his mum about my dad, Mrs Smith told me one night that they used to be good friends years ago. She never said why they fell out though, I don't really want to know. It'd be better if we could just get away from here.

Secondary school isn't all that bad, the classes are a bit more interesting and my English teacher is always trying to get me to enter competitions. I appreciate his help and all that but sometimes I feel it's a bit too much. The other kids take the piss out of me because of it. I get enough grief from them as it is. I don't mind if it's after school but not while everyone is there. He reckons I need to be pushed, I can push myself though, I don't need his help all the time. Anyway, I'm one of the only kids that actually does their homework.

Sitting eating a sandwich on a bit of grass that's in the playground I remember I need to bring Mrs Smith some milk. She can't walk so well anymore, she seems a bit frightened to go out. It's a bit sad really, she never used to be frightened to go out. I don't blame her though, I don't even like going out too late myself. I still go round there and chat with her, I don't read her books so much anymore, I've read them all about ten times already. She's a nice lady, she cares about mum too which not many people do.

To be honest it ain't easy to come to terms with your mum being a smackhead, junkie or whatever else people call her. It was easier when I didn't really understand, people say I didn't know, I knew something was wrong, but I just ignored it. When you're a kid like that what are you supposed to do? She's my mum, she was and is the only person I really have. They don't know her, they don't know that deep down she's a good person. I don't worry about it much anymore, I'm just trying to help her survive, keep myself surviving too so hopefully I can be someone.

The afternoon is long and boring, same old classes, nothing interesting. I overhear some of them talking about what they're going to do at the weekend. I'm jealous, I wish I could go out like they do. I can go out, I just don't have no one to go out with. I spend most of my weekends reading books, making sure my mother has eaten or hasn't overdosed and sitting in the park in the evenings watching over the city and thinking. I come up with scenarios in my head where one of them will come over and talk to me and ask me if I want to come. It's never happened.

The end of the day comes and everyone leaves the building. I've stayed behind because I want to finish something off that I'm writing. It's easier to do it here, I don't feel so on edge. There's another girl in here too doing some work. She doesn't live on our estate, I don't know where she lives. She keeps herself to herself, a bit like me. She seems to work hard but I've never spoken to her before. I've wanted to, but I can't get the courage, bit like when I used to see Joe's sister, the words just won't come out, I know I'll go red.

She gets up and leaves in a hurry, not even noticing I'm there. She's left a pen on her desk, it looks quite expensive, I call after her but she doesn't hear me. I pick the pen up and put it in my pocket, I'll give it to her tomorrow, it'll give me a chance to try and talk to her, I might even make a new friend. I just want someone to talk to sometimes, someone other than Mrs Smith. I'd talk about anything, I really, really just want to be able to talk to someone.

My mind has gone blank and I can't think anymore so I get up and leave. There's no one else around in the school, even the teachers have gone.

Walking back along the road home I see Joe and his friends sitting on a wall. Some of them are staring at me, I look away but I hear Joe tell them to not bother me. Passing the woods I remember the times we used to play in there, how our lives have ended up so different in the space of only a few years. The fat kid has grown up, the fat has turned to muscle and everyone likes him. The kid with no dad still has no dad and his mum is still a junkie.

I go into the shop and get the milk and walk over to Mrs Smith's house. It takes her a while to open the door these days because her legs aren't so good. When she opens the door she looks a bit wary for some reason.

"What's the matter?"

"Nothing, love. Some kids have been knocking on the door and running away. They do it late at night sometimes and it's a bit frightening."

"Which kids?"

"They run away, how am I supposed to know?"

I put the milk in her fridge and make her cup of tea like I always do when I go round to see her. We sit down in her living room. She's a lot quieter than normal.

"There's something up, what's the matter?"

"I've got something I need to tell you, but you can't tell your mother. You have to promise me that."

"Even if I told her she wouldn't remember."

"Promise me."

"I promise, what is it?"

"I found out where your father is."

"What?"

"Someone helped me find him, I know where he lives but that's all I know. I'm going to give you the address. If you don't want it you can throw it away. If you want to go and see him, you need to think about it hard first. I have no idea what sort of person he is and I don't know what sort of person you think he is but you could end up disappointed, he might not even want to see you."

She passes me a folded up piece of paper she has written the address on.

"Why?"

"I always said I wasn't gonna let you turn out like your mother, you're like a grandchild to me. I know you try to look after her and I know you hurt inside. I'm getting old, I'll probably be around for a few years yet but I wanted to do something that would really help you. You can choose to go and look for him or not but I think if you make that decision you will feel better."

"Thank you, you mean a lot to me too, don't go talking about death just yet."

"What are you going to do?"

"I don't know, I need to think about it, like you said he might not even want to see me, I don't even know if I want to see him either. I sort of blame him for how we've ended up."

"It's up to you, I just wanted to give you the choice."

Something I've been searching for all my life is there in my hand and I don't know how I feel about it. I feel as though I want to cry but I don't know why, I don't know if it's because I'm sad, happy or relieved. One thing I do know is that he's not a singer in Spain. I've no idea where I got that from. The address doesn't tell me anything either, just where he lives, and I don't recognise the place. I put the piece of paper into my bag, I'll think about it later.

We sit in silence, I can see she is getting old. She was one of them people that I never thought would get old, she always looked the same until recently. Her and mum have been the only two people that have always been in my life. If she goes I don't know how I would be able to cope. Another thing to worry about. If she gets too done up how will I be able to look after them both, she'll have to go into a home or something. All these things I'm thinking about I shouldn't be, I'm still a kid, I should be out enjoying myself.

I leave in a bad mood. I should be happy but I only feel anger. I know she is trying to help me but she's given me a decision I don't really want to make, it was easier having an imaginary dad. Now it is real I have no idea what I will do. I shouldn't be angry at her, I should be angry at him for walking out. I should be angry at mum for leading a life so fucked up that I want to escape it. I should be angry at all the kids who have teased me for not having a dad because it's made me want one even more.

There are cars outside the house, I can't be bothered to go in now. Not with all those weirdos that she has around in there. I'll end up fighting with one of them. I feel in my pockets to see if there's any money, there's enough to go and get some chips. I can sit in there and talk to Georgie for a while, he doesn't ask any questions and at least he makes me laugh with his crazy ideas about the world. I might ask him about Joe's mum, anything to take my mind off the piece of paper in my bag.

"I no see that old lady anymore, why she doesn't go out?"

"She's got old, Georgie, she can't do as much as she used to. You should go and see her, she'd like the company."

"Where I get the time to go and see people? All I do is make chips, sausages, feed you people."

"I'm sure you're not skint though, 'us people' give you our money for your chips. Take yourself away on holiday, mate. You might not be so angry then."

"I'm not angry, I just tell it like it is. You like my new kebab machine?"

Kebab machines all look the same to me but I need to humour him if I want to hang around for a bit, he might get the hump and tell me to leave.

"Yeah, it's lovely, never seen one like it. I'll have the usual."

"Why you no want a kebab?"

"Because you're charging 8 quid for one and I haven't got 8 quid to spend on it."

"How much you got?"

"About 4 quid."

"Okay, I make you 4 pound kebab, you can try then you tell other people my kebabs are good."

"Who am I gonna tell?"

"Tell your friends at school."

"Go on, then, I'll have one. How long have you been open here George?"

"Nearly 20 years. Why you want to know?"

"Just wondering. Bet you've met some characters."

"Characters? I meet a lot of crazy people, fat people, people who eat to much, drunk people. They give me money, that's all I care about."

"Nice. Did you know my dad?"

"No, I know him if I see him but he and your mother they never came here."

"I heard that crazy woman who's always on the balcony put a brick through your window because you kept giving her boy chips."

"Haha, who told you that? She said she would put a brick through the window, so I told the kid not to come anymore. I thought he was your friend?"

"He used to be, we don't really talk now."

"Good, his mother is a bad woman."

"She ain't so bad, bit like you really, always pissed off with people."

"Still cheeky. Here, your kebab. You can eat it here but I have something I need to do so can't talk."

He hands over the kebab, it looks like it's an 8 quid kebab, he wouldn't want me to think he's being kind.

I finish up my kebab and walk off home. There doesn't seem to be anyone there now. I open the door and walk into the smoky hallway. There's beer cans all across the living room, foil on the coffee table she bought last year. She doesn't even try and hide it anymore. Leaves it to me to clean up when I get back. Every time I tell her she needs to clean up after herself she brings up that time she had to clean up after me when I threw my chips all over the place when I was a kid. Big difference between chips and heroin stained foil.

After cleaning up I shut my door and lock it. I don't want to be disturbed tonight. I sit down on my bed and take out the piece of paper with the address written on. Now I have this I can't even begin to imagine what he is like, all the fantasies I used to have are now just blank, my brain unable to work as it usually does. He could be absolutely anyone, I might even have seen him before but I would never have known.

If I go and see him what if he doesn't want to see me? What if he is nothing like the person I want him to be? He could be just like my mother, then I'd have two fuck ups for parents and I'd know about it. He's probably got another family, what will they think of me? How will I even be able to go through with it? Do I just walk up to the door and knock on it, I don't know what he looks like. He might have done well for himself, if he has, he's not going to want me turning up on his doorstep spoiling it all for him.

If I don't go then I will always wonder what would happen if I did go. I'll be wondering for the rest of my life what this man was really like. He might want me to turn up, he could be wondering what I'm like, every knock on the door hoping that it's me. I ain't got many people, I know I keep saying it, but I ain't, Mrs Smith won't be around for that long, mum could be dead tomorrow and it wouldn't surprise me, it'd kill me but it wouldn't surprise me. I need someone I can look up to. I just don't know if this man is someone that I can look up to.

My mind is a complete muddle. I often feel lonely but right at this moment I feel like there is no one else in the world but me. Or there is everyone else but I'm invisible. I have no idea what the right choice is, I don't even think I have the courage to go and see him anyway. All I want is to be able to talk to someone who doesn't know me, just let it all out, I don't want someone rescuing me or helping me, I just want them to listen. I put my hand in my pocket and take out the pen the girl left, I must remember to give it to her tomorrow.

As I'm finally drifting off to sleep I hear the door slam. There are no voices so she must be alone. At least she's made it through the day. That's what my life has come too, I'm 15 years old and I'm left wondering every night if my mum will still be alive. If you gave me the chance to be someone else, to be taken away from here right at this moment, I would take it. I love her, but I'm not sure I can handle this anymore. I don't want to be that kid with a junkie mum who sleeps with men to pay for her habit.

Why's Do They Call Him Liar?

I was talking to my friend the other night and she was laughing at me for staying behind after school to do work. It's okay for her, she's one of them people that finds everything easy, if she didn't do her homework all year she'd still end up passing all of her exams. Wish it was that easy for me! I just want to get this finished and go home, dad said he was going to cook dinner for us tonight. Not that he's a good cook or anything, it's just nice when me, mum and him sit around the table for dinner and talk. Not much more to do.

Dad was talking about taking us away to Greece in the summer. I can't wait for that, I hope he doesn't change his mind, I doubt it, he usually does what he says. We haven't been away for a few years now. He's always been working when I've been off school and mum doesn't want to go away without him. The girl I walk home with sometimes was saying I must be rich to be going away on a holiday like that. We aren't rich, they just work hard and try to do things when they have the time. I just laugh, I don't care what anyone thinks. Even if they were rich, what's the problem?

I get on with most people but I wouldn't say I have many close friends here at this school. Most of my friends went to other schools when we left primary school. The best friend I made here left last year because her mum got a new job somewhere. I was pretty gutted but I suppose things like that happen sometimes. I can't wait to leave school, not because I don't like it but because I want to go to college and do A levels and then go to university. I've made up my mind on that, mum always says I'm optimistic! Don't see what's wrong with that either.

That kid everyone says is a liar is sitting in the room too. I wonder why they call him that? I asked someone and they said he made things up, when I asked them what, they just said they didn't know, someone else had told them. I never see him talking to anyone apart from the English teacher so I don't know how he'd even be able to tell lies! It's bad really, when someone calls you something at school it always sticks, it doesn't matter if no one really knows why people are calling them that.

I know he has problems with his mum, everyone knows that. We all see her about at the weekends or sometimes I've seen her when I'm on my way home from school. Last time I seen her she looked really ill. I can't imagine having to go home to someone like that every night. You'd think people might try and support him really but they won't, some of the things I've heard the other kids say are terrible. I'm not any better either though am I? I'm sitting in a room with him here at the moment and I haven't said anything to him, I'm trying to make it look like I haven't even noticed him.

What can I say to him if I do talk to him? He might think I'm being a bit weird just talking to him for no reason. He looks busy anyway. I suppose I could ask him about what he's writing, it isn't often people stay behind to do their homework. I wonder if he's even noticed me? I'm getting distracted now. I only came here because it's quiet and I'd get my work done quickly. I'm being nosey too, he has enough people talking about him behind his back, never mind me sitting here with him in the room trying to figure out what he's really like!

He might want to talk to me though. I've noticed him look back a couple of times when he's thinking I'm concentrating when I'm really sitting here holding a pen and not actually doing anything. Well, I am, I'm trying to work out why they call him Liar and whether I should talk to him or not. I'll just go and ask him what he's writing about, that would be easiest. I can't really make any judgements on someone I've never spoken to. If he is as weird as people say he is, I'll just make an excuse and walk away.

Oh shit! I forgot I'm supposed to go and meet mum at five so we can go and do some shopping before dinner. I haven't even done half of the work I wanted to, I don't have the time to try and talk to him now. Oh well, I'll just have to keep wondering. He just looked back again, I feel sorry for him. I get the feeling he just wants someone to talk to or be nice to him. I'll find some time at break or something to talk to him. I don't think he goes the same way home as me so it won't be then. Come on, you've got to go or mum'll start moaning.

Walking past him he has pages and pages of things he's written down. His handwriting looks quite neat as well. I swear his hand was shaking too, I wish I didn't have to go so quickly. He'll probably think I'm just like everyone else now, I probably should have at least said goodbye, just a little acknowledgement that I know he exists. That sounds a bit bad doesn't it? A bit arrogant maybe? Oh I don't know, I'll definitely find the time to speak to him soon.

Philosophers, Girls and Fathers

You know when you really want to say something to someone but you can't, especially when they are talking to someone else. You feel as though they won't hear you or what you have to say isn't important as what the other person is saying so you change your mind. That's how I feel most of the time, now even more. The girl whose pen I have is stood a few metres in front of me talking to some other kid. I'm standing here, face red already, my head telling me you can do it another time. The thing is, I only want to give her back her pen but for some reason I'm thinking some kind of life changing event is going to happen.

The other kid walks away and she starts to walk off in the other direction, I just stand there, unable to move. My face is still burning and I feel dizzy, why do I feel like this? She's gone, another chance missed. This is the third time today I've tried to give her back her pen and every time I've failed. I don't know why I feel so low about myself, feel as though nobody would want anything to do with me. I'm still clutching on to the pen in my pocket, I don't want to take it out in case she sees and thinks I've nicked it.

I'll try again tomorrow, I can't do it today, it isn't the right time, she's probably busy anyway. I walk off back to my class. English, one of the few things I enjoy. I'm entering a competition and I want to get the story I'm writing perfect. Even though what I have written is good, the teacher is still not happy with it. He keeps telling me I can do better, I'm not pushing myself enough. He says if I work hard enough I've got a career in writing. I remember the stories I used to write as a kid, that one I never told mum but wanted to every single day I came home from school. It was ridiculous, I don't know what was going on in my head back then.

It's still my escape though. I can take myself away from mum, dad, the place I live in, that I have no friends. I can build a world where no one can touch me, where I'm the one everyone else wants to be, not the one nobody wants to be. I try to tell my own stories through the stuff I write at home, but I've never let the teacher see it, I think it might be a bit too much for him, drugs, prostitute mothers and runaway dads. If I let him see it it'd be admitting the problems I have too, I try to keep them to myself, I know I have them, I just don't want anyone else to talk about it.

I've written something about me when I'm older, I've gone off travelling around the world. The teacher said I should write something different, take myself away from my surroundings, place myself somewhere else, somewhere I've always wanted to go, it doesn't matter where. I'm thinking about going to see where this address is after school. It's stopping me from concentrating on what I'm writing.

The kid sitting next to me is a bit weird, how come all the strange kids and the misfits always end up next to each other? He's just sitting there in a daze not writing anything, I don't think I've ever seen him do anything but no one ever bothers him. They just leave him to whatever it is he thinks about, the teachers and the other kids. The other kids are scared of him because they think he's a bit mental.

"What you writing about? Every time I see you, you're writing something."

"Just for that competition Mr Jones was talking about, he wants me to enter it."

"I can tell you a story, you can write it down and then we'll split the winnings. We can be rich then innit."

"I don't think you win any money."

"What's the point then, man? You're wasting your time, you need to be doing this for some money."

"Don't really bother me, I just like writing."

He shakes his head and then goes back into whatever world it was he briefly came out of. Like he is no longer aware of me sitting next to him. I wish I could switch off like that. He comes back out of it again and looks at me.

"Seriously though, I have a story, will you write it for me? I don't want no money, I just want it down on a piece of paper, so I can look at it sometimes, remind myself and that."

"Remind yourself of what?"

"I'll tell you later. You're that kid innit?"

"Which one?"

"The one whose mum is on smack, I go past your house every day. Last time I see her she was looking kinda ill."

"Don't worry about my mum."

"Nah man, I'm not saying nothing bad about her, I'm just saying she wasn't looking to good. Listen, man, I ain't got nothing against you, I don't even know you, so I ain't gonna judge, I ain't even gonna judge your mum 'coz I don't know her either, do you know what I mean?"

"She's been ill recently, think she's got the flu or something."

"Yeah the flu. Look man, I like you, you ain't like all these other kids, you got ambition..."

"How do you know I've got ambition?"

"You're sitting here writing, all these other kids ain't doing nothing, they're just pretending. See me, I ain't pretending, I'm just not doing nothing, I don't care. When I leave school I don't know what I'm going to do, and if I'm honest, at the moment, I don't really care. I come to school because I have to, not because I want to. I know what they all say about you, how you're a liar and how you make shit up because you ain't got any friends. Don't listen to them people, man. They're idiots, they ain't got nothing better to do than talk about other people."

"I aint gonna lie I thought you was a bit dumb that's why you don't talk."

"I ain't dumb, I just can't be bothered."

"What about what you want me to write down for you?"

"That's it, write about you! That's what I'm saying, you've got a story, you are a fucking story, you don't have to make anything up."

"I told one kid some stories when I was in primary school, that was it. I thought he never told anyone. My story, if it is even a fucking story, is shit, no one wants to hear about it."

"Whatever, it's up to you."

And that was it, back off into his own world. There's no way I'm going to write down my own story, not even if it was just him that read it. I don't even know this guy and he's giving me advice on how to live, they should do philosophy at this school, he might pay attention then. For the rest of the lesson I can't think properly, all the ideas I had before talking to him have gone. I'll have to sit down tonight and try and do something, hopefully there will be nobody at home, if not I might just go round Mrs Smith's and do it.

Leaving the classroom I see the girl whose pen I have. This time I don't even hesitate.

"You left your pen, yesterday when you stayed behind to do some work. I picked it up so I could give it back to you."

"Oh, thank you! I didn't even realise I'd lost it."

"No worries, what were you staying behind to do?"

"Just some work, it's noisy at home so it's easier for me to do it here. Sorry, I have to go, I need to be somewhere after school."

"Okay, see you later. Look after your pen!"

"Bye…"

She looks at me funny, why does everyone look at me funny? I thought I played that quite cool. She must think I'm some kind of weirdo just like the rest of them do. She ain't from the estate though so I don't think she knows that much about me, she doesn't seem to talk to anyone else. At least I spoke to someone, even those few seconds made me feel a bit better about myself. I turn around and start to walk home.

"Jay, can I talk to you for a minute?" It's our head of year.

"Yeah?"

"Come to my office, it's quieter there." I follow her to her office.

"How have things been for you recently?"

"How do you mean?"

"Some of your teachers have been saying that you are very distant. You do your work, but that's it, they all say you have potential but there seems to be something stopping you. I'd like to find out what that is."

"I do my work, what else do you want me to do?"

"Push yourself, aim higher, try and achieve something with your life when you leave here. How's things at home?"

"Not this again…"

"It's my job to care about my students…"

"I told you last time there's nothing wrong at home, then that woman still came round and started asking my mum questions. What happens at my house ain't got nothing to do with you lot. I come to school and do my work, that's all you need to worry about."

"It's not all we have to worry about, we have a duty of care…"

"Everything is fine, seriously, don't worry about it. Don't send no one round there either, you'll be wasting your time."

"I'm just asking. Your English teacher says you have serious potential, if you apply yourself you could probably go to university, not many of our pupils go on to do that, if I can help you get there, I'll do all I can."

"We'll see. I ain't becoming your pet project though."

"Just have a think about trying a bit harder. You can go now."

"Thank you."

What is it with all these people involving themselves in my life? It has nothing to do with them. Walking out of the school gate the kid who sat next to me in class is standing by the gates, he nods his head at me, I don't think I've ever seen him nod at anyone before. This guy. I don't think he's going to leave me alone. Of all the people he has to choose to talk to he has chosen me. I want someone to talk to but not him. I haven't got the time for people that think they are philosophers. I've got the piece of paper in my pocket with the address on it, I take it out and have a look and head towards the tube station.

The teacher talking to me has made me not want to go home. I know she's right and if I go straight home it will confirm she is right, everything is wrong at home, it's completely fucked up, but I don't want to give her that. I ain't going to go and knock on his door, I'm just going to go and see where it is, if I can see what kind of place he lives in I might be able to work out what kind of person he is, then I can make a decision to see if he would want me in his life or not.

Sitting on the tube is like escaping out of the bubble. There's people from every part of life, people with their big briefcases going to the cities, geezers with ladders and paint stained overalls, from all over the city. When you live on an estate like I do, it's like it becomes your whole life, like there's nothing outside of it, people not from where you are from are thought of as strange even though they only live over the road. Maybe that's why there's so many bitter people, we don't know nothing else and it ain't a big community really.

No one looks at each other when you're on it. The geezer opposite me keeps looking up but when I catch his eyes he looks straight back down again, or looks up like he's looking at the advert for some kind of death insurance above my head. There's a crazy man on our carriage as well, talking to himself, sometimes shouting, but none of the other people take any notice, like he isn't even there, even though he's crazy and might do something mad. The people waiting on the platform can see that he's crazy and they move along to another carriage, but the people already on it just sit there, like they've got special powers and if they ignore him he won't do nothing.

The train stops and the train driver starts to talk over the loudspeaker, telling everyone the train has been delayed because of a signal failure. The crazy man starts shouting at the loudspeaker, saying he's going to punch it up. I look around at the other people and they still just sit there, pretending to do something. The crazy man gets up and walks through the doors to another carriage. People exchange glances and then get back to pretending to do something again, the only time they'll make eye contact on the tube.

The train finally pulls into the station and I get off. I know where I'm going because I looked it up on an A-Z we have in the house. I'm good with maps, I only need to look at it once and know where I'm going. The road I'm looking for is not far from the station anyway, I've only got to turn once. I feel like I'm so far away from home, I don't know this area at all, it isn't even that far away but to me it could be in a different city. It seems like there is more money round here, there are shops you wouldn't get where we live.

Turning on to the road my heart starts to beat faster. Every man I pass I wonder if it is him or not. He wouldn't know what I look like and I wouldn't know what he looked like. I've never even seen a picture of him. I looked through mum's drawers when she was passed out once and I couldn't find anything, just pictures of me and her when I was a baby. One of them was cut in half, I guess he was in that one when it was taken. I know I'm looking for number 34 but I'm on the wrong side of the road because these are all odd numbers.

I'm kind of worried too, if someone sees me walking slowly down the road they might think I'm up to no good. The houses are all terraced, attached to each other. They all seem well kept, the small gardens at the front have bright flowers. The doors all look freshly painted, the cars outside the front of the houses look expensive. I don't think it's a rich man's area but it ain't like back home. I pass number 30 and my heart beats quicker. I don't want anyone to come out of the door, I don't even know what I'm going to do when I pass it.

The door is bright red, there is a flower box on the window full of purple flowers. The gate is closed, the curtains are all drawn too so I can't see inside. There is a parking space empty just outside the house, I wonder if it is his, if it is he must have gone somewhere. I'm regretting coming, what was I expecting to see? I took my anger out on that teacher and instead of listening to her and going home and doing some work, I'm here. I carry on walking past and down to the end of the road. I want to turn back and look one last time, there's nobody else on the road but I make movements as if I've forgotten something and turn around so I can pass it again, probably looking even more suspicious.

Reaching the house I stop and look around, checking to make sure there definitely isn't anyone there. I open the gate carefully trying not to make any noise, it makes a loud creak. No one seems to be inside. I walk up to the flower box and pick one of the purple flowers, I do it carefully, trying not to disturb any of the others. I leave quickly, taking out one of my schoolbooks as I walk, putting the flower into the book and pressing it down. Once I'd got here I didn't want to leave with nothing. I wanted to feel like my trip had been worth something.

Sitting back on the train I feel more relaxed. Maybe because there ain't any crazy people this time and the carriage is empty, but I know if I don't go back again, I have something that belongs to him in some way. I hope it belongs to him anyway. Seeing where he lives, I don't know if we're the same kind of people. It looks like the kind of place a family would live in, he wouldn't want a kid from his past turning up on his doorstep. Especially one like me.

Homework

There's nothing for miles around, just fields, no houses, no people. It's like how they show it in the movies. One night I stayed up late, I watched this film about a man who went travelling around the world. He hired a car in America and drove from one coast to the other. Where I'm standing now, it looks exactly like it did in the film. The corn in the fields is swaying. I think I can see a house in the distance but I'm not sure. Imagine what it must be like to live out here? No one to bother you, just yourself, peace and quiet.

I get back in the car and carry on driving. When I've reached the other side of the country where will I go then? Maybe I could head down south to Mexico, keep going all the way down to South America, writing in my diary as I go. Ever since I saw that film it's what I have wanted to do and now I'm here doing it. Even the dark clouds that are forming on the horizon look spectacular, not like at home when you see clouds and you start to feel down. There are a few rain drops in the air, I'll have to find somewhere to hide from the rain. That must be a building over there.

Pushing the corn aside as I pass them, I can't really see where I'm going, it's just a general direction. I don't care if I get lost, I'll only get wet, I have enough money to pay for the car if it gets stolen. Who would steal it out here anyway. The corn gives way to an open field, just grass. There is definitely a building on the other side of it. I look up, the clouds seem to be swirling, they are tall, rising up higher than I've ever seen any cloud before. The air is wet, it's going to be a big storm. What if I just stay out here? What's the worst that can happen?

I reach the building, it's a barn of some kind. It looks old, the wood is falling away in places. There are more raindrops, I push at the door and it falls down, I jump back. It's just old, no one must have been here for a long time. Inside there's a table, an old chair that's missing one of its legs and an old typewriter, it's rusty, if I touch it I think it will fall apart. There's no paper, I wonder how long all this has been here? Who would even live out here? The last town I passed was hours back. They had the right idea staying out here.

There's a loud thunder clap. The clouds are above the house now, I can still see blue sky back in the direction I came from. I sit down on the fallen door and watch as the dark clouds move quickly above the house. The raindrops sound heavy on the old wood. I hope it doesn't collapse, it won't, this won't be the first storm it's been through. There's a flash of lightening and another bang. The rain begins to fall in sheets, the wind whistling in where there used to be pieces of glass in the windows. I want to go out in it.

I step outside, soaked within a few seconds. I forgot I left the top of the car open, it'll be drenched. It doesn't matter. I hold my arms out and look up at the clouds. Anyone watching would be wondering what this crazy person is doing. I walk out to the middle of the field and turn around towards the barn or house or whatever it is. I wish I had a camera, it's one of those scenes you could only dream up. The dark clouds going back to the horizon, a battered, old barn with broken windows with a solitary tree standing next to it. This is why I left home, to see things like this.

I run back to the barn, my temporary madness having left, I realise I'm standing in the middle of a field during a thunder storm. The rain has broken the heat, I start to feel cold. I notice there's an old blanket in the corner. I pick it up and look at it, it doesn't seem to dirty. I take off my shirt and hang it on the old chair, hoping its three legs will hold it up. I wrap the blanket around myself and sit down against the wall facing the open doorway. The rain is starting to ease off now, I don't really want to leave, I could live somewhere like this.

There's a rainbow over the corn fields. I don't need any pots of gold! Peace, quiet, nature, that's why I came out here. My shirt is still soaked, I pick it up and wring it out, the water falls to the floor. I remember I still have the blanket wrapped around me, I can't take it with me. Even if nobody has been here for years, I want to leave it as I found it, hopefully someday someone else will come across it. I place it back in the corner I found it in. I look at the typewriter, maybe someone used to come out here to write. I pick up the door, it's heavy but I can lift it, I manage to balance it so it covers the doorway, it'll probably fall down in the next storm.

I reach the corn field and look back at the barn one more time. I don't think anyone would believe me if I told them this. They probably wouldn't even be interested, it's not that exciting really is it? At least I know there is someone else out there that has shared it with me, they knew the magic of being somewhere they can be at peace with themselves. I wonder what they wrote on that typewriter? I'll never know. I'd better get back to the car, hopefully there'll be more places like this along the way.

Is She Dead?

It's hot outside, the flat is even hotter. Freezing in the winter, baking in the summer. She hasn't been back for nearly four days now. I like the quiet, but I know I need to go and look for her soon. She's either in some crack house or more unlikely gone somewhere to cold turkey. That's just wishful thinking, if she was going to do that she'd do it at home, I'd have to watch her go through the torment, almost like she's putting on a show, looking for my sympathy, even though I'm the one who takes care of her.

I'll give her until six and then I'll go and look to see if I can find her. When this happens I become less enthusiastic each time, looking for her but not really wanting to find her, going to places she probably won't be at because at least I can clear my conscious and tell myself I've looked for her. Looking out over the green the kids are playing football, a scene that will be the same in twenty years' time. I wonder if I'll be looking over it in twenty years? I doubt she will be, but then I doubt she has ever even looked out the window.

I threw the piece of paper away last week. I know where he lives, if I want to go I know where it is. The paper felt like a weight in my pocket, every time I looked at it, it was telling me to go back. I haven't even opened the book I put the flower in. I feel stupid for taking it. Even looking at it would make me feel embarrassed. Even if it is his, I don't know him, and at this point would I ever be able to get to know him? Would I be able to not blame him for the way everything has turned out? I'm not sure. I can't hate, I'm not spiteful.

It's just gone six. I lock the door and walk towards one of the other blocks, it's somewhere new she's been going to recently. I don't think she'll be there, but it's close and I need to start somewhere. The lift in the block is broken, I walk up ten flights of stairs, helping an old lady with her shopping as she struggles up them. She complains there aren't any gentleman left anymore, all these foreigners coming over, they don't care about anyone but themselves. She takes a packet of cakes out of her shopping trolley and gives me one. I try to refuse but she insists.

Reaching the tenth floor I see the door I need to knock on. The worst part of all this, you don't know who is going to open it, most of them recognise me now though. I bang on the door hard, I can see a shadow through the glass as someone looks through the spyhole. The door opens a crack and a thin faced woman looks through it. "She ain't here. I haven't seen her for days. Sorry love. You shouldn't be coming round to these places, just let her come back on her own." She shuts the door without waiting for my reply.

Outside the block there is a man sitting on the floor, I'm not sure if he is drunk or on drugs, I give him the cake, he looks at it unimpressed and throws it away. Food is obviously not important to him. I walk towards the high street, a flat above one of the shops where her friend lives. She might know where she is. I just want to know she's alive, if she's alive I'll probably stop looking. The high street is busy even though it is late evening, people still out in their shorts and t-shirts, white pasty arms and legs that might not see the sun again this year, foreigners in jumpers and long trousers looking at them like they're crazy because they don't think it's hot.

111

I knock on the door and the woman answers, she tells me to come in.

"I don't know where she is Jay, I'm clean, I have been for a few months. I can't hang around with them people anymore."

"You any idea where she might be?"

"She could be anywhere. She kept talking about sorting herself out recently but last time I saw her she looked worse than I've ever seen her but you probably know that yourself. I want to help her, but I can't put myself at risk, you need to understand that."

The woman in front of me doesn't look like the one who used to come round to our flat. Her skin seems brighter, her eyes don't look dead, the dark rings have almost faded away. Her smile feels warm too, not the fake acknowledgement I used to get. The last time I came here it was full of beer cans and foil, now it's neat and tidy, the coffee table spotless apart from an ashtray. The windows are wide open, she's watching some film. I feel some admiration for her, I also feel bad for how I used to have such hatred towards her, blaming her for all mum's problems.

"Do you want a drink? I've got some coke in the fridge, or tea or coffee if you want it?"

"Go on then, I'll have a coke."

She goes into the fridge which is full of food, mostly salad stuff. She's gone completely into her healthy living.

"How's things? I've obviously not seen you for a while."

"Things could be better, if I'm honest I'm close to giving up on her."

"I don't blame you, I've been there myself, my kids don't talk to me anymore but I'm trying my best to show them I'm doing the right thing this time. Your mum loves you though, you know that?"

"She has a funny way of showing it, I hardly see her anymore, even when I do she barely speaks. She has no idea what I'm doing at school, I doubt she even cares. I'm 15 years old and I feel like I'm 30, I fend for myself, it's not easy."

"She'll realise one day. You need to give her some support, you're all she's got."

"All she's got is the drugs. Do you know what it's like to have to go to school and listen to people talk about your mum being a crackhead and a smackhead and people saying they saw her getting into cars. Asking me what it's like to have a mum that's a whore? If I'm all she's got she wouldn't be doing this would she!"

"Look, I can't moralise. I've done everything she's done. She's probably never told you but she ain't had any easy life, you need to understand..."

"She doesn't need to take it out on me, she doesn't even try. At least you've given it a go."

"It ain't been easy, every day is a struggle for me at the moment, but I hang in there."

"Listen, I've got to go, I appreciate you talking to me but sitting here I see her, I see what she could be and it's too difficult for me."

"Okay, I understand. Look after yourself. You could try down on that estate by the station. She used to go there a lot. It's on the top floor of the tower block, you'll know which house it is when you see it. If you ever want to come round and talk I'm here if you want."

"Thanks, I'm pleased for you, I'll be honest, I never really liked you but you seem different."

She reaches out to hug me as I leave, there's a tear in her eye. It doesn't feel fake, just strange for someone who I don't really know to react like that. Passing all the people standing outside the bars and pubs I feel contempt for them. I don't know any of them but I hate them. My anger is becoming more and more directed towards other people, not just myself. They are laughing and joking, some of them singing, maybe it's because I want that too, just to be happy, just to be able to escape, even if it is for a few hours. They've got friends as well, people they go out and enjoy themselves with, something I haven't got. I'm wandering round crack houses looking for my mother.

The lifts are working in this block but they smell of piss. The doors open and she was right, I know straight away which flat it is. There's a large metal gate over the door. I have little hesitation this time, ringing the bell, the anger has taken away my fear. The man I see at our house sometimes, the one who frightened me as a kid opens it, I suspect he knew it was me somehow. My hatred and anger multiplies, this man is everything I despise, I see him as the person who has taken my mother away from me.

"Where is she?"

"She's dead."

"What?"

"Dead. D. E. A. D., brown bread. You ain't going to get to see her anymore, you won't have to see me anymore either, I expect you'll be happy at that!"

"If she's dead then where is she?"

"Fuck should I know? Probably at the hospital or wherever they take dead people."

"How do you know she's dead?"

"Because I do."

I hit him, as hard as I can. He falls backwards in surprise then stands up again and laughs.

"I'm not going to hit you, you're a kid. How does it feel to have no mum? Or is it just the same as it has always been?"

I run down the stairs, all twenty floors. At the bottom I rest against a wall, sliding down it. Now what? I've been expecting this but now it's happened what am I supposed to do? I don't even know where she is. I can either go to the hospital or go to the police. One of them must know if someone has died. I don't feel sad, just numb, I'm not sure I even believe it. I feel guilty, some nights I had wished she was never around and now she's gone, I'll never see her alive again. How did it even happen?

Picking myself up off the floor I make my way to the hospital, I don't want to see the police. I ask at the reception for her, they say there is no one there with her name. I leave, the only thing I can do now is go to the police, if she's dead they must know. As I walk back down the high street I see her friend on the other side, it's almost empty now, she waves me over.

"I know where she is."

"She's dead!"

"What? She's not dead, I spoke to her half an hour ago. She's at a friend's house, she's detoxing, she went cold turkey."

"What? That prick told me she was dead. Are you sure?"

"I'm sure, I rang a few people up after you left. She doesn't want to see you tonight, she's not in a good way. I went to the house but you weren't there. Wait another two days, if you want to stay with me you can."

"It's okay, I'll be okay on my own, I'm used to it."

"It's up to you, if you need anything come and see me. I'll come and pick you up in a couple of days and we'll go and see her together."

"If you could come round tomorrow, I'd appreciate that, I'm a bit lonely, if you've got things to do it doesn't matter though."

"I'll come round tomorrow, it's fine, I'll cook you a bit of dinner if you want."

"Yeah, we could go to the chip shop, whatever."

"I'll cook something, I'm sure you'd like something a bit different."

"See you tomorrow."

"Oh wait! Your mum told me to give you some money, she'll sort me out when she's better. There's a hundred quid there."

"You can't give me a hundred quid. What about yourself?"

"I wouldn't give it to you if I didn't have it, I'd saved up some money and I get my social tomorrow. She's going to give it back to me, it ain't a problem."

She's getting clean! Five minutes ago I thought she was dead and now I hear she's doing something good for once. I feel guilty, even though I was sad there was a part of me that was relieved when I thought she was gone. Walking back to the flat I feel as though I'm lighter, if she really has managed to get off the drugs things might be different, I'd forgive everything just to have my mum back for the rest of my life. I'm still scared to get excited though. I don't want to be disappointed. This has to be the most fucked up day of my life, and that isn't an easy choice, maybe that kid was right, I should write it all down.

I sit at the bus stop waiting for the night bus. I've been here for over half an hour and still nothing has come along. It's been enough time to change my mind but I'm not going to. I'm going to get on the bus back up to where my dad lives. It's night time, they'll probably be asleep but I just want to see if there is even a light on. I feel like something is dragging me back there, even with the day I've just had, I can't get that house out of my mind. Throwing the paper away hasn't helped, I have to go back and look.

The city seems a different place at night, like it's sad. All those people you don't notice during the day, they're all visible now. People wrapped up in blankets on doorsteps, alcoholics on benches sharing bottles and cans. Drunk people staggering home from wherever they've been during the evening. It's like the people are the city's tears and they're only released at night. The bus passes a girl under a bridge, she only has a cardboard box, that's probably all she owns. For everything I've been through I'm glad I have somewhere to live, I could easily be her. I wonder how she got there?

I get off the bus at the next stop. I'm not going to go tonight, there's no reason for me to go and see him, it's a waste of time. I walk back towards where the girl with the cardboard box is sitting.

"Are you hungry?"

"No, I ate earlier, but I'm thirsty."

"What do you want to drink?"

"Coke"

"I'll be back in two minutes."

I go into the 24 hour shop next to the bridge and buy her a can of Coke and take it back to her.

"Thanks, I appreciate it."

"How old are you?"

"16."

"If I'm bothering you tell me to go away but I saw you from the bus and thought you might need some company."

"Haha, come in, this is my house, it's not very nice, there's a few rats, but make yourself comfortable."

"I was going to say it could be worse, but that probably wouldn't be a good thing to say."

"I'm alive at least."

"How comes you're here? What happened?"

"I ran away from home. I live up north, I lived up north. I was bored and thought I'd run away to the bright lights. It isn't really so bright down here is it?"

"Nah, those postcards are a lie, we don't all live like that. What are you going to do? Don't you have anywhere you can go, family and that?"

"I've been here for a year already."

"What? Living like this?"

"Yep, you get used to it after a while, do miss sleeping in a bed though. Hunger isn't good either, sometimes people give me money, most of the time they just ignore me. They probably just think I'm going to spend it on drink and drugs but I don't do either. I don't have the money to go home anyway."

"It's probably a stupid question, but what are you going to do?"

"No idea, sometimes I think about going back home but I'm so ashamed of running away I'm scared to go back."

"I've never told anyone this but my mum is an addict, I've brought myself up, I've thought about running away like you so many times . Everyone knows but I've never actually said those words to anyone but myself."

"Do you live with her?"

"Yeah, when she comes home. She's supposed to be getting clean at the moment. I ain't sure if I believe it or not, I doubt she'll last very long. I've wanted to run away so many times. It fucking kills me watching her destroy herself, I don't give a fuck what anyone says about her, I just hate seeing her do what she does. If I run away though she'd end up dead, besides where am I going to go? Any bright lights up north?"

"Haha, it isn't that bad up there. I never had too bad a life, my mum and dad gave me everything I wanted. We lived in a nice house, I did well at school. I was stupid to run away but like I said now I'm too scared to go back home."

"Imagine how your mother must feel. She doesn't know where you are, you could be dead for all she knows. I bet every time someone knocks on the door she's hoping it's you."

"It is fucked up here, I hate it."

"Go home then, I don't like preaching but you ran away for a stupid reason, you have a mother and father that care about you, you can't just run away because you're bored."

"How am I going to get home with no money?"

"Here take this, if you want to go home you can. If you don't at least do something useful with it."

"You know I probably won't go home?"

"Don't worry about it. I can go home and sleep in my own bed, there's something I can eat in the fridge and I have someone I can go to if I need anything. You don't, just take it. If you don't use it to go home you'll always know you had the chance. I'm going, I need to get home."

Will She Do It?

I don't think I can remember a time when I've seen her like this. She still looks thin but her eyes aren't glazed over anymore, there's brightness to them, as though she really is alive. Even her skin looks lighter, not as pale and pasty as it was before. When she is looking at me I feel as though she really is looking at me, not looking right through me. We still haven't spoken, I'm just sitting next to her holding her hand, it is shaking slightly, I don't know if it is through nerves or because she is still getting all the shit out of her system.

"My legs are still sore, but I feel better. I didn't want you to come when I was really ill, I didn't want you to see me like that."

"I've probably seen you in a lot worse states, mum. I've thought you were dead more than a few times."

"Sorry..." she says sheepishly.

"Just stay clean, that's all I'm worried about. I can't take you like that anymore, it's killing me. Whatever has happened before is done."

"I'm going to do whatever I can, I promise you."

"Just get through this and then take it from there. You look better but I can tell you're still ill. At least I can have a proper conversation with you."

"Yeah, I know, I've missed my son." She smiles as she says it.

"I'm going to go, you just stay here for a couple of weeks, you can't go back there until you feel strong enough."

"I know. You need to go to see Mrs Smith, she's going to lend us some money until I'm better and can give it back to her."

"Okay, I'll get it on my way home, I haven't seen her for a while, I feel a bit bad."

"She said she's seen you but thought you didn't want to see her. She cares about you, spend a little bit of time with her."

"I will, I will, don't worry."

"When I've got through this I'm going to take us away for a week. Go to the seaside if you want?"

"Yeah, I'd love to. I feel bad mum, but I feel like we need to get to know each other."

"I know, go on, go, I'll be okay, just make sure you look after yourself. I'll phone home tomorrow at about 4."

"See you later mum, please don't fuck this up."

I hug her for longer than I ever have and leave, not able to look at her, my eyes red, fighting back the tears. Still a bit doubtful yet excited. I know her too well to have too much hope, but if I don't have any hope what's the point? I shut the door and let out a big sigh, I'll walk home, it'll take about an hour but I can go along the backstreets, I want to enjoy my relief and hope, walking helps me to enjoy it more. Seeing kids out with their parents, people outside pubs in the sun, I don't hate them anymore, they make me smile.

I see Joe on the balcony outside his door, there are two policeman too, his mum is shouting at them. Joe has his head bowed down. God help who ever has led him astray. Seeing him makes me think of beaches and the sea, how close I was to going when we were kids, the disappointment and anger when I couldn't go. Now it looks like I have another chance, just not going to let my hopes get too high, not like last time, I don't want to feel that disappointment. I'm still smiling as I knock on Mrs Smith's door.

"I thought you'd forgot all about me"

"Nah, I could never do that, I've just been a bit distracted, that's all. You know about mum?"

"Yeah, she told me before she was going to do it. I didn't really think she would but I spoke to her this morning and she sounds like a child again. I hope she keeps it up."

"So do I, I ain't going to get too excited though, we'll see what happens. She reckons she's going to take me away somewhere when she feels better."

"Sounds nice, where you going to go?"

"To the seaside somewhere."

"You'll both enjoy that, to be honest I wish she'd take you both away and not come back. That kid that you used to hang around with when you were younger, I've seen him hanging round outside the block with some dodgy people. I reckon he's selling drugs."

"Haha, how would you know he's selling drugs?"

"I know a lot more than you think. Here's your money, I've told her not to worry about giving it back. Make sure you feed yourself properly. You can come here whenever you want..." Her eyes look at me longingly, I feel bad for neglecting to go and see her.

"I will. I'll stay a bit now anyway, I haven't got anything to do."

"I've been wanting to ask you..."

"Yeah, I went, I didn't knock on the door though, I just looked at the house. I don't think I want anything to do with him. It's too difficult, I don't know how he would take it, I don't even know whether I want it either. For the moment it's best just to leave it. If he comes to find me that would be better."

"I doubt there's much chance of that love, but it's your choice. I only wanted to give you the chance to make a decision."

"I have something I want to ask you."

"Go on..."

"What happened to mum that she turned out the way she did?"

"I really don't know, I'm not sure anyone knows but her. Something happened, I know that, she changed too much, too quickly. I've never asked her, she doesn't have many real friends, if I asked I was scared she'd try and push away from me, I just want her to feel I'm always there and I'm not going to put any pressure on her."

"I don't want to ask her either."

125

We sit and talk for hours, talking about when I was a kid. Mrs Smith telling stories of what it was like when she first came here, how bad she thinks it is now. I don't think it is that bad, maybe I'm just used to it. I'm getting the feeling that she's starting to give up, even though I haven't seen her much lately, the thought of her not being here scares me, she's been one of the few constants in my life. When mum isn't around I can go to her. Perhaps I don't appreciate enough what she has done for both of us.

I stay over at Mrs Smith's, we talk until late, eventually I fall asleep on her sofa and she leaves me there. Waking up early in the morning I let myself out leaving her asleep. I go to the park and sit up on the hill, my usual place of misery is now a place of optimism. I used to think everyone else out there was happy, but looking out over the city now, I realise that I wasn't the only one that was miserable, there must be so many people in positions like mine, I hope that they will get some kind of hope too.

On my way back home I stop at the shop to buy some things so I can clean up the house. I struggle down the road with bags of cleaning stuff and a mop and bucket. I hear someone call out at me from behind.

"Do you need a hand with that?" it's that girl whose pen I picked up.

"Nah, I'm fine. I didn't know you lived round here?"

"Yeah, I live just down the road from you, on that estate across the road from where the green is on yours."

"How comes I never see you around much?"

"Don't know, I don't really go over to where you live that much, most of my mates live on my own estate. You sure you don't need a hand? I'm going back your way."

"If you could take the two bags I can carry the mop and bucket."

She carries the bags back to my front door for me. We walk in an awkward silence, sometimes asking stupid questions to try and start a conversation. When we reach the door she's still holding the bags, I don't want her to come in, I don't want her to see I have almost nothing.

"I have to do some things, thanks for carrying this stuff home for me, it was good of you."

"No worries, look if you're ever bored, come to my house and knock for me. It'd be good to go out and do something sometime."

"Yeah, okay then, next Saturday?"

"Yeah, see you later, enjoy cleaning."

"How do you know I'm going to be cleaning?"

"I've just been carrying a big bag of cleaning stuff for you!"

"Oh yeah, I'll try, laters."

I didn't make too much of a mess of that. For once, things really do seem to be looking up! I sit down in the living room for a few minutes before starting my clean up. It's not even that messy, I just want to scrub it clean, a bit like washing away the past. I don't know if it'll work but I can try. It begins to rain outside, I open the windows wide to allow the fresh air to come in, it feels like I'm moving into a new home.

I wash all the floors and clear out the fridge. I clean the windows too and then realise it has been pointless because of the rain. Underneath the sofa I find an old newspaper from 20 years ago. It's stained brown and the pages feel as though they will fall apart. I read through it, taking a break from the cleaning and taking a trip back in time. The newspaper has a picture of a man on the front page, a serial killer that had been caught. I don't recognise his name but for some reason his face seems familiar. After finishing the paper I throw it into a rubbish bag, nothing in it worth keeping.

The part I am dreading the most is the one I've left until the end. Opening her door it's tidy but I know that I'm going to have to go through everything. I don't want to look through her stuff but I don't want there to be anything left she can use when she comes home. She'll understand, she probably doesn't remember she owns half of this stuff anyway. I open the bedside drawer and start taking the things out and putting them on the bed. There is a picture of me and her as a baby, I place it to the side.

I find a pipe made out of a miniature whisky bottle, I don't even want to pick it up, it's almost black, it's a part of what has made life so difficult for me. I throw it in the rubbish bag, making sure it goes to the bottom of the bag so I won't have to look at it again. I put everything back inside the drawer, it looks like it was all the way I had found it. My guilt at looking through her stuff has faded having found the pipe. The black rubbish bag is on the rug that was there even when I was a kid, still with the small blood stains on it, I fold it up and put it outside the front door.

I go through all the cupboards and drawers but find nothing else. Looking through the final cupboard I find a square box, the ones you keep photographs in. I open it up and look through them, most of them are tinted brown like the newspaper, people with haircuts that have gone out of fashion. There is one of a man smiling, he has a bushy moustache, the bottom of the picture has been cut away but it looks like he is holding someone or something. I don't recognise him but he looks a bit like my mum.

There's another photo, mum holding a baby, I assume it's me, there is a man next to her as she sits on a hospital bed. They are both smiling, close together. I've never known her to talk about any relatives that are men, it must be my father. The picture is black and white but I can see how young he looks, how young both of them look. Mum looks happy, he has a smile but it looks forced. I wonder how it must have felt to have a kid you didn't really want. Would I run away if I was in his place? Maybe not, but I know what it's like to grow up without a father.

I take the picture and put it under my pillow. The box doesn't look like it has been opened for a long time, if she asks about it, I'll just say I don't know where the picture went. If we go away I want to ask her anyway, there are things I need to know, things she has to know too. Now I have seen the picture I feel less like I want to meet him, he looks like he was just a kid who made a mistake, there is no real connection between us. All the lies I told Joe about him and now I know what he looked like I almost feel disappointed, I want to believe those lies.

Clean

It's the first time I've been out since I decided to do it. I can feel the cool breeze of the morning on my skin, the sun on my face. I'd forgotten what it felt like to feel even the simplest of things, things everyone else sees as normal are like new experiences. I'm finding it hard to walk with my head up, avoiding eye contact with anyone that passes, worried they recognise me or I've done something to them in the past, it's like a weight is holding my head down, lifting it ain't easy, an old woman I pass smiles at me and says good morning, I can't look that bad.

The shopkeeper doesn't take any notice of me as I give him the money for a newspaper and a packet of fags, I smile but get nothing in return, I shouldn't have expected anything but it's knocked my confidence again. Walking back to my friend's house I still feel a bit shaky, my legs are still sore but the worst of it is over. Someone said to me it was the easiest part, if that was easy I ain't sure how I'm gonna be able to get through the next part, living life as a normal person. I'll just have to take it as it comes, see what happens.

Seeing the boy was hard, all the guilt, shame and hurt, it all came at once. Looking at him was difficult, no matter how much I'd told myself I'd let him down before, it isn't real until you actually feel them emotions. His encouragement masked all his disappointment in me, I'd always felt I wasn't wanted, that no one cared for me, but seeing his eyes and face light up when he realised I was clean, I knew he cared, the one person that does care is the one that has suffered the worst. I'm still scared, scared that I'm going to let him down again.

Being over the worst of it I've begun to start thinking a bit more positively, something I ain't done in years. If I can sort my shit out, I might be able to go to night school or something, try and do something for myself. It's the motivation part that is the hardest for me, motivation and confidence. They used to say I was clever at school but I didn't have enough confidence, that if I pushed myself then I'd be able to do something with my life. I don't know where I'm supposed to be able to get that confidence from though. It's only been a week, take things slowly.

Looking through the paper I can see how disconnected from the world I have been. I've not read one in years, I've not even watched television in years. People they are writing about I have no idea who they are but they seem to be very famous. I used to love reading the paper, I always wanted to know what was going on in the world. It looks like I'm going to have to start again, I feel like an old woman who hasn't left her house in years. Looking at the fashion column I think about all the things I'd be able to buy if I can keep this up.

There's a box on the floor with one of them labels that has 'fragile' written on it. That's how I feel, completely fragile, like if anything touched me I'd break. The last few days I haven't been craving, I've enjoyed not having to wake up and go out to get money, not having to worry about how long it's going to take me to make money and how long it is before I can get what I need. I'm still fragile though, I'm aware it probably wouldn't take much for me to throw the last week away, walk out the door and find somewhere to score.

I'm looking forward to being able to take the boy away for a few days. We can go somewhere nice, he's always wanted to go to the seaside. That's the small goal I've set for myself, the first goal, I want to achieve that and then move on, find other goals when each one is complete. A few days by the sea will do me good too, I'll be able to get away from the estate, away from all the people that judged me and will still judge me. I might even move down there one day, get away from this place for good, once he's old enough to do his own thing.

I keep getting flash backs in my mind of all the stupid things I've done, physically cringing as I think about them. I try to think about the future and the good things that will come of it but they keep coming into my head, uninvited, thoughts that I don't want, don't need at the moment. They will always be at the back of mind until I face them but I ain't sure if I really do want to face them or not. If I don't face them, then what? Will I be able to go through life not running away? There ain't many places I have left to hide, if I do run away again, hide form it all, I think it'll be my last hiding place.

All of these thoughts and feelings, both good and bad, it's all new to me, I don't know how I'm supposed to handle it. In a sick way I'm mourning the life I'm trying to walk away from. All the pain it has caused me, all that pain it has caused him, I still have a longing for it. Most of it was madness, insanity, darkness, sadness but after only a few days I'm starting to miss it.

It must be the boredom, or is it because it's all I've known for the last 15 years? I'm trying, I really am, but this is really fucking hard.

Is This a Date?

What if I say something stupid? I just want a friend but I really like her, why am I so nervous? I keep looking in the mirror, each time I look I change my mind on how I look, first time I think I look okay, second time I think I look stupid. I want to walk out the door but something keeps holding me back and I have to go back and look in the mirror. I feel like when I get outside everyone will be looking at me, I don't know why they will be looking at me because I don't even look that different to what I normally do. This is stupid, I need to go.

No one is looking at me. I cut across the back of the estate to get to the one she lives on quicker, now I'm thinking it's a bad idea, I should have gone the longer way around so it would take longer, a bit more time for me to prepare myself and think. What do I even need to think about though? This is mad, why am I feeling like this. When I press the buzzer what am I going to say? What if her old man answers and he doesn't know I'm coming? Maybe I should just leave it, say I felt sick when I see her next. She did tell me to come round though so he must know.

Standing here looking at the buzzer, I make sure nobody above can see me, they'd be wondering why this idiot is just standing there with his finger hovering over a button but not pressing it. I put my finger on the round silver button, it feels cold, I can't press it, I just can't find that last bit of force to push it down. I put my hand back in my pocket, I'll go for a walk around the block and then come back again. I keep close to the walls, if she was looking out a window she wouldn't be able to see me.

Back in front of the door and the buzzer again. Maybe I should go around one more time. No, I'll press it, how can pressing a button be so difficult. I put my finger back on the button and push. It makes a long ringing sound. Please answer first time so I don't have to press it again. I'm waiting for an angry, deep voice asking who it is daring to come to their house. There's no voice, the door clicks, I pull on the handle and it opens. That was easier than I thought it would be. There's a lift but I take the stairs, it'll give me a bit longer to get ready.

The door is already open. I walk up to it and knock softly, a small man appears from a door.

"Hello mate, in the living room, just in there. You want a tea or coffee? There's a few beers in the fridge if you want one."

"I'm okay thanks."

"Just tell her to get you something if you want it."

He goes back inside the room he came out of shutting the door. I walk into the room and she's sitting on a big sofa watching the television. I sit down on an armchair.

"Did he just offer you a beer?"

"Haha, yeah!"

"Never offers me one! I just want to finish watching this and then we can go out for a walk or something if you want?"

"Yeah, that'd be good. What you watching?"

"Some programme about a guy that rents a car in New York and then drives across America, it's really interesting. It'll be over in a minute."

"Yeah? I'd love to do that!"

"Really? Maybe one day we'll have the chance to do it together! Haha."

I hope she hasn't seen my face turn red. I don't think she'd being serious anyway. I don't really watch programmes like this, it makes me feel jealous of the person that's doing them. It's finished now anyway.

"I'll just go and get ready, be five minutes. Do you want a drink or anything?"

"Nah, I'm fine."

I always feel out of place in anywhere that isn't home or Mrs Smith's. It's like I shouldn't really be here, uncomfortable, scared to touch anything in case I accidently break it. I hope she doesn't take too long, I don't want her dad to come back out, I don't know what to say to him even though he seems quite nice. I hear a door open. Please be her. It's not, it's her dad. He walks into the room and sits down where she was sitting and starts turning the channels over on the tele.

"Where you two off to then?"

"Just going for a walk, I think."

"You live over on Shakespeare don't you? Used to know a few people over there but they've moved away, there was a nice little pub there. Always used to be an old boy in there that never said anything, funny old place."

"Yeah."

He looks at me like I should have said more, I want to say something else but I don't know what to say.

"Anyway, I've got to get ready for work. I'll probably see you some other time."

"Yeah, nice to meet you."

I hear another door open and she walks into the room. She smiles at me as I get up, I can't wait to get out of here.

"What was he talking to you about?"

"Nothing really, said he used to go over to where I lived a lot."

"Yeah, he did. He's okay, you don't have to be shy in front of him."

"Where's your mum?"

"She's at work, she doesn't get back until the evening, if we come back later you might see her then."

"What does she do?"

"She works with special needs kids in a school. She isn't a proper teacher, she's like an assistant."

"Oh, okay."

"Where we going then?"

"Could just go down the park or something and have a walk about. Unless you want to go up town."

"DAD! Lend us a tenner!"

"You mean give you a tenner. Here's twenty, go and enjoy yourselves. Write your mum a note to let her know you'll be back late."

We walk down the stairs and out the main door. I'm trying to think of something to say but my mind is blank. I laugh to myself, she looks at me like I'm crazy. We cut back across my estate to get to the bus stop, I still can't think of anything to say to her. This is bad, I must seem like a complete idiot. How comes I could talk to her the other day? Every time I come up with something I just think it's stupid so don't say anything. We reach the bus stop, I've forgotten I have hardly any money, I feel the coins in my pocket, I'm not sure if it's enough to get on the bus.

"I'll get the bus fares, it might be one of them old buses anyway, the man doesn't always come round for tickets on them."

"I have got money..."

"I know you have, my dad just gave me twenty quid, might as well use it."

One of the old buses pulls up, there's no doors on the back of it. The conductor doesn't look very interested, I doubt he's going to collect the fares, there's only another two people on the bus. We go up the stairs and sit at the front. I sit next to her but don't want to sit too close so half of my leg is hanging over the edge of the seat. She moves closer to the side of the bus. Is that to give me more space or because she thinks I'm too close to her? I move over a bit so my leg is flat against the seat. She looks at me and smiles. I feel warm all over.

"Where do you want to go?"

"Not sure really, where do you want to go?"

"Walk along the river? My dad used to take me when I was kid, I used to love looking at all the buildings along there."

"Yeah, sounds good."

"We can go up to the shops if you want but it'll probably be really crowded."

"Nah, it's fine."

I kind of wanted to go up to the shops on Oxford Street. Not because I wanted to buy anything, but because I wanted people to see me walking around with her. I wouldn't see anyone that I know but it'd make me feel good. Stupid! You spend all your life telling yourself you don't care what people think and now you want to try and impress people you don't know and don't even care about you. If only she knew what was going on in my head at the moment! She'd think I'm a complete lunatic, she'd never want to go anywhere with me.

The bus pulls up at the bridge. Big Ben and the Houses of Parliament opposite. All the tourists running around taking pictures with big cameras. Neither of us take a second glance at the two famous buildings as we walk down the steps to the walkway that runs by the river. So much for it being not crowded, there's people everywhere. I don't mind though because I still can't think of anything to say to her, at least here it's noisy and crowded, I don't feel so awkward. Further up the path there are less people.

"Let's sit down here for a bit."

We sit down on the bench. I look out across the river as though I'm looking for something in particular, or just taking in the scenery.

"I don't know what to say to you…"

"Me either…"

"I don't mean that in a bad way. Everyone must ask you about your mum so I'm trying to think of something to say that doesn't involve her."

"Haha, to be honest, I don't talk to that many people. In primary school kids used to tease me all the time, in secondary school they pretty much leave me alone because I just keep myself to myself. I'm shy though, always have been."

"Do you ever think about what you want to do when you've finished school?"

"More recently now that mum seems better. I don't know, I've always wanted to be a writer but I don't know how to go about it. I don't really like school, I ain't bad at it, I just think it's boring."

"You could go to university."

"I've thought about that, but all the bad memories I have of home, I'd still be scared to leave it. I write about leaving and travelling and seeing the world and achieving things but they all just seem like dreams, I don't know if I'd actually take the opportunity if I had it. It sounds stupid, I don't know if I'm explaining myself properly anyway."

"I understand. I've never read anything you've written, you should give me some of it, I'd like to read it. What have you written recently?"

"It was something about going to America. I've always wanted to do it, I used to spend hours looking at an atlas when I was a kid, the old lady that used to look after me had one. I would look at the maps and try and imagine what it was like in the different places. I don't know if that's what it is really like but I try. I just want to take a car and drive from one side to the other, like that geezer on the programme you were watching earlier."

"Do it then."

"I've no money and I'm only 15, what do I do? Just pack my bags and go? I wouldn't be able to leave mum here on her own anyway."

"Why not? At some point you need to take some responsibility for yourself, you can't let her control your life. I'm not saying that because I think she's a bad person, I reckon she'd probably want you to go and do what you want with your life. If you don't you'll probably regret it."

"I don't know, if I wasn't about, I think she might relapse. She seems better but if I'm honest, every time I go home I still get nervous when I put the key in the door. I'd like to just forget about it for the day. What do you want to do?"

"I want to go to university, become a teacher I think. Don't really want to move away or anything like that though. I always hear people saying 'I need to get out of here' like it's going to change them, I don't think it will. It's up to you, if you want to do something then you need to want to make it happen."

"I suppose."

"I want to ask you something, you don't have to tell me if you don't want to. Some of the kids at school call you 'Liar'. Why?"

"Fuck, I thought people had stopped calling me that. When I was at primary school, I didn't have any friends except for one kid, you've probably seen him at school, his name's Joe. I made some shit up and told him, I lied to him. I don't really want to go into what it was but he told other kids and now they all just think I talk rubbish."

"Do you?"

"Do you know what it's like to be so lonely you'd do anything for a friend? People say I didn't know what my mum was up to, maybe I didn't know exactly but I knew something wasn't normal. You know your life is all fucked up, so you create a new reality. I was only 9, I had no friends and I wanted people to like me. It was a way for me to escape too, when I was telling him my dad was a singer I believed it, for those few minutes I wasn't going to go home that night to find my mum passed out or strange men walking out of my house."

"I believe you. Everyone tells lies as a kid. I just find it strange they still call you 'Liar'."

"I don't know either, I barely talk to anyone at school."

"Don't worry about it. Come on, let's go and get something to eat. I'll pay for it."

I don't know where all that just came from. She just listened. She hardly said anything, just listened to what I said and didn't make any judgement. Now I feel like I don't want to stop talking. We walk through the back

142

streets to find something to eat, talking as we walk, mostly nonsense, nothing important. Wondering what the people in the big houses do, talking about people at school, laughing about teachers. I think it's the first time in my life I feel relaxed with someone. Like I'm safe, happy and safe.

Other People's Problems

Mum is sitting on the sofa, she tells me about her day and then asks me about mine. I just tell her we went up town and walked around for a bit, didn't do anything too exciting. She rolls her eyes and looks up at the ceiling. She says dad has gone to the pub after work so he won't be home until later. She's watching some rubbish on the tele. I leave her to it and go and sit in my room. My feet are sore after walking so far. I feel tired but a happy kind of tired, where you know you've done something nice.

It was a really nice day, I don't go out that often. I couldn't believe dad gave me £20! I didn't realise Jay was able to talk so much. It's funny, I knew he wanted to say something when we were walking but I didn't know what to do to make him feel more comfortable. I was looking at him while he was talking to me, his eyes were bright, you can tell he's clever but there's a sadness in his face. It's like something inside of him is trying to escape but it doesn't know how. I knew I should have chosen to do psychology next year!

Is it bad to feel sorry for someone? I feel like feeling sorry for him is wrong, but I can't help it. He's a nice boy, I really do like him but that's it, he's just a friend. I don't know, I made a judgement about him before I even met him and as much as I want to ignore what I used to think, I can't, there's always this doubt in my mind. I want to put myself in his position but I just can't do it, I don't have anything that even compares to him. My mum and dad always do the best for me, I don't ever want for things, I don't have many friends but that's my choice. How can I empathise?

When we came back from town earlier, I watched him walk home, he looked happy, happier than I have ever seen him. I know I'm part of that, his mum getting better is too, but I'm worried he thinks it's going to be something more and I'll end up having to hurt him. There's a distance about him that makes me feel as though you're never going to properly know him. I suppose he's just protecting himself because he's been let down. We'll see, even if I can encourage him to do something he likes, that'll be something.

Labels stick, I have no reason to not believe him when he's speaking but he's been given a name by the other kids and every time I'm with him, it's still there in the back of my mind. It's crazy. Am I a bad person? I wish I had known him when he was smaller, it might change how I think, or I might never have made friends with him. As much as I want to do something that feels significant for him I don't think I can. I'll just keep trying to be his friend, it's a little bit of support, I don't care what other people think either.

Thinking about what he was saying about leaving, maybe that would be a good idea. Not him, I mean me. Go somewhere different if I end up going to university. I don't hate it here but I suppose it would be nice to see another part of the country. Depends on how well I do in my exams as well though, if I want to get into a decent university I'll have to start studying a bit more than I do. I'm not really sure where I'd want to go though. There's still plenty of time to think about all that. Every time my mind drifts to something it keeps coming back to him. I wish he'd never picked that pen up!

I can't get some of the things he said out of my head. I don't understand why things would be so bad that you'd have to make things up. I like to dream, everyone does don't they? When I was a kid I used to pretend my room was a palace and that I was a princess. When I went outside and saw my friends I didn't ever think it was real. It's different though, you can't tell people you live in a palace when they can see your house anyway. I never asked him about his dad, I should be grateful that mine never left me.

I wonder if he still does it? Still makes things up in his mind and then starts to believe them. Did he really believe them when he was a kid? This is driving me crazy. Sometimes I wish I didn't really care about people. At least that way you don't have to worry all the time, or you don't have to try and work out what is going on in someone's head. You can hurt someone and not care. That wouldn't be better though. Those people probably do care, they just try to pretend they don't. Can I rescue everyone I come across though? I can't do that.

This is bad, I genuinely do care about him and I hope that he's okay but I'm not sure I can hang around with him anymore. We had a nice day, a really nice day but I've ended up sitting on my bed tormenting myself about how I can help or whether I'm able to help him. I'll be doing what every other person in his life has done to him but I can't get mixed up in his life, I've spent a few hours with him and I feel completely drained. I hope he finds some proper friends, I really do, I'm a terrible person but I can't do this, not even as a friend.

Let's Go to the Beach

I don't know if this is what I expected. I like it, the air is different to London, it's fresh, especially in the mornings when you wake up and go for a walk. I could live here, it would be better if it was somewhere abroad though, the sand here isn't very yellow. We're here for another week, we've already been here for a week. We're staying in some bed and breakfast, the room is small but it's comfortable. The woman who owns it is a bit strict, she doesn't like us coming back too late, but at least I've finally made it here.

Mum has been clean for almost two months now. She struggled at first but she seems to be getting better, she smiles more, she listens to what I have to say. She's talking about getting herself a job when she gets back to London, she says she'll save up enough money to take us both somewhere abroad if I do well in my exams next year. I still worry, I still have doubts that she is going to keep it all up, I'm just trying to make the most of this time we have together, just in case it does go all wrong in the end.

I feel nervous around her, she isn't the same person I knew before. Not in a bad way, just, she's my mother and at 15 years old I'm only just starting to get to know her properly. She is more shy than I ever thought she was, she's also a lot more clever than I thought, she even helps me with some of my homework. I don't know, it's like she's got younger since she's got off the drugs, like she's gone back to my own age and starting to grow up again, feeling and seeing all the things she missed the first time.

I've left mum in the bed and breakfast while she takes a nap. It's the afternoon, there are loads of kids on the beach playing and messing about in the sea. I smile to myself and remember how much I wanted to go when I was a kid. I stop by one of the stalls selling ice cream and buy myself one. It's a small achievement but eating an ice cream while walking along a beach is something I thought I would never be able to do. The happy families along the beach don't bother me, not now, I've accepted it's only ever going to be me and mum.

I've been working hard at school, I even won one of the competitions the teacher entered me into. They put the story in the school magazine and I had to read it out in front of half the school. I went completely red but they clapped at the end.

The teachers at school are telling me I should start thinking about going to college and university. Mum came to the parents' evening at the end of the last school year. Even the teachers looked shocked to see her, I don't think any of them even knew what she looked like. They kept telling her I had potential but I need to try and fulfil it. Since then she keeps telling me I need to try harder. I think I'm trying hard enough, it's strange her trying to push me, I like it, but it just feels strange.

Mum is sitting outside in the back garden of the bed and breakfast reading a book. I sit down next to her and she smiles.

"Where did you get yourself off to?"

"Just went for a walk along the beach. I'm not looking forward to going back really."

"Me neither, but we can't stay here, you need to go to school and I need to make some money for us."

"What are you going to do?"

"I have no idea, I don't really have much on my C.V. I was talking to the woman in the social and she said I can go on some courses, it might help. I'll just try and get a job cleaning."

"What did you want to be when you were a kid?"

"Haha, I wanted to be everything. I used to love reading, I wanted to be a writer for a little while and then I changed my mind and wanted to be a nurse, when I used to go round Mrs Smith's house and she told me about New Zealand I wanted to go exploring the world."

"Still time…"

"We'll have to get some money first."

"I want to ask you something mum, but I don't want you to get upset."

"What?"

"Mrs Smith said you changed when you were a kid, you were really good at school but you suddenly changed. What happened?"

"She knows love but I think she just wanted you to ask me yourself. I'm not upset."

"So, what happened?"

"My dad, your grandad, he used to drink a lot. He would come home in the evening's and start knocking mum about. This was when I was really small, then one day he just left. Mum didn't say anything about it so I didn't ask, I was glad he'd left, I didn't love him."

"Why didn't your mum call the police?"

"People didn't back then, you just got on with it. Once he'd gone that was it, she was a lot happier and I was a lot happier. When I was a teenager I started to think about him more and more, I had been too young to know him and even after what he had done to mum I still wanted to find out what he was like."

"Did you look for him?"

"Yeah, I went to look for him. Mum knew where he lived, the address was in a book in her room, I copied it down and then went to find him. He had another family, I knocked on his door, when I told him who I was he told me he'd never wanted me and didn't want anything to do with me, I wasn't his daughter, I had no father. Even though I knew he might not want to see me, it hurt me, feeling like he didn't want me made me want to try and make him want me. I kept going round to his house and waiting outside, one day he came out and slapped me and told me to go home."

"Did you ever see him again?"

"No, I never saw him again. I told mum what I had been doing and she went mad. Told me I was stupid and after everything she had done for me why would I go and find him. She said I'd ruined her happiness by going to see him, so I felt even more worthless. After that she had a breakdown, she barely spoke to me, I tried to make it up to her even though I didn't think I was wrong but she wasn't having it, she started drinking all the time and would hit me when she was drunk. I was old enough to fight back but I couldn't, she was my mum."

"Mrs Smith said you two seemed happy…"

"Maybe from someone on the outside looking in we were but it wasn't happy, I used to dread coming home because I didn't know how drunk she'd be, I'd hope she was so drunk she'd fallen asleep or couldn't get up so she wouldn't hit me. I started to not go home because I was scared. I tried to find my dad and ended up losing my mum too. I was staying at people's houses that I didn't really know, one night someone offered me some heroin, they said it was like being wrapped in cotton wool. I stopped for a while when I met your dad and had you. When he ran off it was another person leaving me, I couldn't cope. Here I am 20 years later."

"I thought something worse had happened to you…"

"It was bad, love. My mum had been a good woman until I went to find him, she changed overnight, she battered me stupid some nights. I lost my mother, my father and your dad."

"I suppose. That's how I've felt though, like I haven't had a mother…"

"I know, I always said I would look after you and wouldn't leave you but the more the drugs took hold, the more I wanted to blank everything out. It's not right what I did, I know that, I'm not trying to justify it."

"What about my dad?"

"Your dad wasn't a bad person, I got pregnant hoping it would mean he'd always be around. He cared for me, I was lonely. He didn't want kids yet, one day he just packed his stuff and went. Another person disappeared on me and I didn't know why."

"Mrs Smith said he was a good person too, but how can you be a good person if you did what he did?"

"He had a good heart, he tried to look after me, it was just too much for him. If you knew him you'd understand why we all thought he was a good person. I know it's hard for you to understand. I understand you probably hate him."

"I don't know him so I don't hate him, I just wish he'd been around. Seeing all the other kids with their dad's when I was a kid hurt me."

"I know it did, it hurt me too, I blamed myself. Everything I've done, the way I've behaved, your father leaving, I can't do anything about that now, I can only try and be a good mother to you from now on. I understand if you can't forgive me, but at least just try."

"I do understand, I just want us to make the best of what we have now. Please don't go back on the drugs mum, I don't think I'd be able to take it if you did."

"I'm trying love, I really am."

I leave her sitting in the garden and go out for another walk. I think I understand but I still feel like I resent her a bit. Her life wasn't easy but that didn't mean she had to make my life hard too, she could have tried harder. I wanted to say that to her but I didn't want to upset her either, I don't want to give her an excuse. It's like I've had to live the life she lived because she wasn't strong enough to cope, she should have done everything she possibly could have to not allow me to live the same childhood as her.

I realise too that she would have felt everything I'm feeling and have felt. She would have resented her dad, she wanted to find him, she had to face rejection too. She saw her mother change into someone else and she didn't know how to handle it. Maybe I'm stronger than I thought because I've just tried to get on with it. If I keep on resenting her we're never going to be able to have a proper relationship. She's here now, she's not on anything and for the first time in my life we're able to talk.

When I get back to the bed and breafast she's lying on her bed, still reading her book. She puts it down when I sit down on my own bed and smiles.

"I hope I haven't upset you."

"No, you haven't, I just wanted some time to think."

"I know."

"I don't hate you mum, but it hurts, it hurts me how I had to grow up, it hurts that everyone used to talk about my mum, it hurts that I never really had a mum. All I want is for you to try your best, I know it ain't going to be easy but I will be there for you and do whatever I can. You know, even if you go back to it I'll still try and help you. I can't just walk away from you, you're the only person I have."

There are tears in her eyes, the feelings she is now feeling are real, I don't think she's used to it. I want her to know though, I want her to realise that I'm not going to be like everyone else in her life and just walk away from

154

her. I'm not going to disappear and I'm not going to judge her or tell her what to do, I just want her to know how I feel. Even though I've said I don't think I can say in words how I do really feel, it's like it's powerful because she is crying but I can still feel the hurt and the pain and the words won't take that away.

"A couple of months back, I went out for a walk, and saw some girl living on the street, she said she was from up north somewhere, she ran away from home. All she had was a cardboard box, no money, nothing to eat, nothing to drink. She told me she still had some hope though, just a little bit. I gave her some money to go home, fuck knows if she went home or not, she probably didn't but I was thinking, that could have been me, I could have walked out on you, but I didn't, I'm still here."

"Thank you."

Tears were still running down her face, I take a tissue from the bathroom and hand it to her, she wipes away the tears. I sit down next to her on the bed and put my arm around her shoulders.

"I'm sorry, I really am."

She lies down on the bed with her face towards the wall and I cover her with a blanket and turn off the lights. Lying on my own bed I can still hear her crying softly. I'm not going to stop her, I think she needs to cry, to let it all out. Eventually she stops and seems to have fallen asleep. When I know she's definitely asleep I cry too, I feel like that little lost kid again, the one whose mum wouldn't let him go to the beach, the one who so desperately wanted a mum to look after him, the one that found her lying on her bed thinking she was dead. After all this time of holding it back and fighting it I let it all out.

I've said it all, I've let it all out but I still don't feel like it's better. I still want to run away, I feel like I'm not good enough, that he doesn't deserve me. He deserves better than this, someone that can look after him properly. I'm like a child, that's how I've felt ever since I stopped using, I've started life all over again and I don't know what I'm doing, I have no idea at all. Everything scares me, I don't know if what I'm doing is right or wrong, I don't have time to be learning again, I want to be strong now, not in a few years.

He seems happy, and I think he understands, but I'm not sure. If he resents me then I don't blame him, I resent my mother and I despise my father. Why should he feel any different? When his dad walked out I tried to make excuses for him, I still try to make excuses for him but now I know what he did was wrong. He might have been young, but I was young too, he left me to deal with it all myself, a young girl with no idea what she was doing, left all on her own to cope. Why do I still make excuses for him? If he hadn't walked out would it all be different?

I keep looking at him and I see someone that is older than they really are. He's fended for himself for all these years, he's seen things that no child should ever see. He's come through all that and he's still here fighting for what he wants in life. He's done better than what I ever could. Does he even need me? I know he worries all the time, worries that I'm going to relapse, go back to the way it was. If I do then he'll walk away, I know he will. I wouldn't blame him either. Why would you keep trying to look after someone that just wants to destroy themselves?

Life hasn't been that bad since I got clean. I enjoy doing the simple things I didn't do before, going for walks, going out to the park, I even went to the zoo once. Things like this, going to the beach with my son for a holiday. I love it, but I still feel like it's all masking something. I'm scared of myself, scared of what I'm capable of, scared that I have no confidence in myself, I don't believe this is how I'm really going to spend the rest of my life, there's always doubt there, a doubt that just won't go away no matter how much I want it to. Or do I really want it to?

How far can someone else take you? I don't think it's far enough. There's a point when you have to want to live your life for yourself and not for someone else. No matter how much you love someone, how much you want what is best for them, it's you that's living your life, they can't save you from the feelings you have every day, they can't hide you away from how much you hate yourself. Your love of them doesn't replicate your love for yourself. I thought it would, I thought getting clean for him would be enough.

Everything I hated about my life before I now have strange cravings for. When I go for walks along the canal in the mornings I see people sitting on the benches drinking at nine in the morning. They're oblivious to everything else, just the can and their escape. I envy them, I didn't think I ever would but I do. I envy that they can sit on that bench so early in the morning, probably not long awake and they can escape from everything that torments them. They don't have to feel it, the numbness, the warm glow that's like a blanket hiding you away.

It was all supposed to be better, easier. I had this dream that we would both live a happy and fulfilled life but I can't see it happening anymore. For him I can see it happening, for me I can't. He'd be better off taking his own path without me dragging him down. Watching him as he sleeps the tears are rolling down my face, I thought I had failed at everything that I ever did but I produced him, that's the one thing that I've given to the world that is a positive. Everything else is a failure, especially myself.

What do I do though? Do I keep on living a lie like this? I'm not going to be able to keep it up much longer. I know it, inside I have already given up, I'm just going along with it all because I feel like that's what I should be doing at the moment. The only thing that is stopping me is the guilt, the guilt and what it will do to him if I leave. I'm trying to persuade myself that he'd be better off without me but I know that it is going to destroy him too. Will he get over it? Do I really have to leave? Is this what I really want?

He thinks I'm happy, he encourages me, tries to get me to do things that I don't have the confidence to do, I know he just wants to see me happy. I'm selfish, the one thing that I have tried to do for someone else isn't working. Maybe I'll give it one more chance when we get back, try my hardest to try and change the way I feel. I'll get a job, the last chance at making something of myself. I have to do it for me though, and that's the part I don't think I'm capable of. If it all goes wrong, if I can't cope, I'll go, for good this time, I won't come back, I wouldn't be able to face him again, ever.

Still Lying

The old fella at the bar has been here since the doors opened this morning. I doubt he's said a word to anyone, the girl behind the bar knows what he wants and fills up his glass as soon as it's empty. There's another fella sitting under the television watching the racing, the Racing Post spread out over his table, swearing as another one of his horses comes in last. The usual afternoon in the pub, you could go back 30 years and you'd have different people but the same characters. I put the two pints down on the table and sigh.

"What you up to this week, John?"

"Fuck all, was supposed to go over to my mum's but she's got the hump, I can't be bothered with her giving me any grief, I'll go over next week. Clare and the kids are doing my head in, that's why I'm in this shithole. What about you?"

"Supposed to be going on some course but I'm going to fuck it off. A mate of mine reckons he can get me a job doing some work as an extra in some film they're doing."

"Yeah? What film's that? Any chance you can get me involved?"

"I ain't sure about that mate, he said he had to pull a few strings to get me a part, I'll ask him but don't go too excited."

"Just ask, I could do with an extra few quid, it's one of the little ones birthdays next week and she'll be onto me for dough."

"Yeah, I'll let you know. Listen, I need to get off, need to see a man about a dog."

"Catch you later, don't forget to ask that geezer, like I said, I could do with the dough."

I shouldn't have just said what I did about that job, there ain't any job. I say things like this all the time and it ends up with me getting in bigger trouble, he won't leave me alone now, always asking if I've spoken to this geezer that doesn't actually exist. I know it's stupid but I can't help myself. I'm not really much different from anyone else around here, I suppose I'm still just trying to make myself stand out even though I don't need to. Maybe I just get so pissed off with how boring life is I make up nonsense to try and make it more exciting.

I cross over the road and walk into the paper shop to get myself a few drinks for when I get home. I've been finding it harder to sleep recently, the only way I'm getting to sleep is to have a few drinks before bed. I've been writing a lot down, it brings back memories that hurt me, at least if I have a few drinks it makes it a bit easier to think about them. I pick up a packet of crisps as well, money is a bit tight at the moment so it'll have to do for dinner, I'd rather get the few cans than get a proper dinner, I'm not that hungry anyway.

The new flat I've got off the council is on the third floor. It isn't that far from where I grew up, you can see it out the kitchen window. Same red door that was there when I was a kid, I don't know who lives in there now, I don't like looking at the place to be honest, I try and avoid it as much as I can. I could have moved somewhere far away, on the other side of the city but I didn't want that, I don't want to be away from here completely.

The flat is a mess, I need to give it a tidy up tomorrow if I can manage to get up early. I need to do something about my motivation, I just can't be bothered to do anything most days, just go to the pub, sit around for a bit and then come back home. The only thing that's keeping me going at the moment is writing. The first few years after she left I wasn't that bad, I didn't need to block it out, I just got on with it, it's just that recently I've been feeling it more and more, when I see kids with their mums on the street it hurts me.

There are kids playing out on the green, they come in earlier these days, their mums don't let them play out as late as they did back when I was a kid. You get a few shady looking characters hanging around at night time, it was different back in the day, there were dodgy people about but they left most of us alone, now they don't seem to care. People used to moan back then but they could moan to each other, these days people hardly know the person living next door.

The first can of the evening is the best one, I enjoy it more when I'm home on my own, I don't really like drinking in the pub, I feel like I have to talk to people I know in there, then I start saying stupid things. It isn't like I'm drunk all the time, I'm not, I just find I've been drinking more and more recently, I really need to sort it out, they reckon it's inherited, I don't believe that but I suppose you can't really take the chance either. It's hard though, that feeling of being relaxed is nice, all your problems don't seem as bad when you've had a few.

My writing book is sitting next to me, I can't look through it when I haven't had a drink or two, I find it hard to read back the things that I've written down, it's like I'm ashamed of it, that it isn't good enough. It's easier to write too, my thoughts go down on the paper easier, I can write how I really feel and how I used to feel without it affecting me too much. It probably sounds like psychobabble. The doctor got me a counsellor I'm supposed to see every week but I struggle to talk to her, she doesn't make me feel comfortable, I'm thinking about not going at all because it's a waste of time.

I've been waiting for two days now. I've no idea where she's gone. I know she's been struggling a bit recently but she usually lets me know where she is. I open the door to her room and see an envelope with my name written on it lying on the bed. There are clothes all over the floor and some of the drawers have been left open. I pick the envelope up and open it, there is some money inside along with a letter, I read the letter. She's gone, never coming back again, I lie back on her bed holding the teddy bear she's left, desperately needing something to hold on to, to hold me.

I think deep down I always knew she'd go at some point, either death or running away. She never could face her problems and I was her biggest problem because she never knew how to look after me. I doubt she's even alive now, there's no way she's made it another ten years, she probably didn't make it ten months. I thought she'd been doing well but I look back and realise it was just blind hope from a naïve kid who didn't really know anything but blind hope, that's how I got through it all them years.

I've been sat at home alone for nearly a week. I've barely eaten, sometimes going to the chip shop when it's dark so that I don't have to see anyone, keeping my head down, hood up. Nobody knows because I haven't told anyone, but I feel like everyone knows, they all knew it was coming, they were the ones who were right, the faith, the belief I had in her has all gone and now they are all laughing at me. Paranoia, fear, loneliness, hatred, hopelessness, abandoned, all those words I was trying to use in my English exam come in useful now.

I can still see that kid walking to the chip shop under the cover of darkness, hiding away from the rest of the world. In a way I'm still that kid, when I go out I don't really want to see anyone, I don't want to talk to them and then when I do have to talk to them I over compensate and start talking complete nonsense, making my life some elaborate fantasy that you know they don't believe anyway. I'm still under that hood, now though, my hood is drink and lies, I don't have to be that little boy when I have them.

I put a few bits of clothes a couple of books into a bag and walk over to Mrs Smith's house. When she opens the door I walk in and fall onto her sofa in exhaustion. I can see her looking down at me in surprise. I manage to pick myself back up again and she walks over to me and hugs me. She doesn't ask what's wrong, she's just there so I can have someone to hold me, someone I can hold. When I let go she tells me to sit down and goes and makes something to eat. At least I feel safe here, she'll wait until I'm ready before asking what's wrong, she always knows when I'm ready.

If it wasn't for her I don't know what would have happened to my life. Don't get me wrong, my life isn't amazing, it's pretty shit, but if it wasn't for her it would be even worse. She did more for me than my mother ever did and she's still here for me. Thing is, when she's gone that's when I really will have nobody left. At least she won't be abandoning me though, knowing her she'll die when I'm ready to cope with it, I can't see me being able to cope with it being anytime soon so I hope she does have a bit longer left.

What's the point in school? I don't have to go anymore, not if I don't want to. I was doing it for her anyway, give her a better life, now she's gone, who am I going to be going for? Myself? Honestly, I don't care about myself enough now, I don't have any motivation to do well, I just want to get by. Mrs Smith wants me to go, but I just can't go in there and face all them people knowing they know I've been abandoned by my mother. I'm confused, things were looking good just a few months ago and now it's all completely hopeless.

I gave it all up, that's why I'm sitting here, living on the same estate I grew up on, having just come back from a dingy little pub to drink the rest of the night away. I didn't see it at the time, you don't. When you've lost everything there's no point looking towards the future because you don't want to face it, everything is grey and the tunnel which leads down to what is going to happen later on in life is even darker, just fading into a darker and darker shade until it's finally completely black. That's probably psychobabble too, but that's the only way I can describe it, try it and you'll know what I'm talking about.

A year to the day she left and there hasn't been any contact at all. Even though she wrote she wasn't going to contact me, I still hoped she would, that she would have a change of heart, that she would realise what she had done. Every time I've heard the phone ring, a knock at the door of Mrs Smith's house, every letter that comes through the door in the morning I look to see if it's for me. I've become more detached from the world outside, scared to go out there, thinking everyone is looking at me, talking about me. I thought this was supposed to be for the best?

She took me in and let me live there. She sorted everything out that needed to be sorted for me. She didn't rush me, she didn't try and make me go out. She did tell me not to have too much hope that she would come back. She knew she wasn't going to, she just didn't want to take away the little bit of hope I had, she wanted me to take it and put it on something else. I don't think she knew what I was going to do with my life but she at least tried to make me look forward, give that tunnel the smallest prick of light at the end of it.

Then there's nothing, nothing I can write about, just the past because there's isn't anything interesting that has happened since. It's been like that for nearly nine years, just getting by from day to day, never having a job because I don't have the confidence to go and meet people I don't know. The doctor gives me sick notes because he says I have depression and the events of my childhood have 'impacted me deeply'. I have friends but they aren't really proper friends, they're just people I see down the pub, it's how I prefer it though, I don't want anyone close to me.

The lights from the blocks of flats have all started to come on, the sun has already set and I'm sitting in the dark of the living room. I get up and walk over to the window and open it, it's a long way down to the green below.

Someone jumped out of a window in one of the blocks a few years back. I wonder how it would feel as you were falling? What would go through your mind? Would there be enough time to regret what you've done? A light comes on in one of the flats opposite, a woman looking out the window too. I wonder what's going through her mind?

Two people walk across the green and sit down on one of the benches. Both dressed in tracksuit bottoms and white t-shirts, looking around every few seconds, on edge. They'll wait there for an hour for someone who said they'd be there in 10 minutes, growing more and more agitated. Even from up here you can feel their frustration. Someone else walking along the path spots them and takes a different route to where ever it is they are going, trying not to make it obvious they've changed their direction.

It's still not late enough for me to go to bed, I look at the plastic bag and see there is only one can left. That's not enough for me to start writing tonight, I'll finish it too quickly and then have nothing left to finish off what I want to write. I open the kitchen cabinet, empty apart from a couple of tins of beans and a small bottle of Jamaican rum Mrs Smith's next door neighbour gave me when she'd come back from visiting her family. Should be enough to get a few pages down, probably enough that I'll end up being awake all night.

I bought a desk last year to put in my room, the writing desk no one else knows about except me. It could tell the story of my life, it's seen me cry, it's seen me angry, seen me laugh at the madness of my life. I put the bottle of rum and the last can down on the top of the desk, the notepad in the middle and lay the pen to the side. It's like a little ritual I have, unless everything is placed perfectly before I start I can't think properly, the untidiness will only distract me from the things I want to recall.

I take one more look out the window before closing the curtains. The two geezers sitting on the bench are still there, tapping their feet, even more agitated than before. I suppose it could be worse, I could be one of those two, living your life for something that never gives back to you. They make me think of mum, remembering the agitation that I used to think was just because she was upset, not because she had a drug habit that controlled every part of her life. I close the curtains, hoping whoever it is they are waiting for will never turn up, wanting them to suffer for no reason other than spite.

I'm looking at her, her hands are shaking, her pale face thin and worn. The cigarette in her hand has burnt right to the end, almost touching her fingers but she doesn't notice. I smile but she doesn't notice, I laugh nervously and she still doesn't pay any attention. Suddenly she winces in pain, the cigarette end burning the two fingers holding it. She throws it onto the floor and stamps on it, then back to staring into space. The way she looks at the wall frightens me, when she's like this she's not my mum, she's just some person, a stranger.

There's a knock at the door, she jumps up suddenly and rushes to the door. There's a brief conversation, the front door shuts and then the door to her room does too. Twenty minutes later she comes out. Her face is still pale but she is smiling at me, she takes me by the hand and walks me to the living room. She lies down on the sofa and motions for me to lie next to her. "Tell me one of them stories you like to tell, sweetheart, I want to hear one." I can't help the smile that comes across my face, my mum is back, even if it is only for a little while.

Sorry

Dear Jay,

I'm sorry, I have to go. All of these years that I've tried to be a mother to you I've failed. I tried to do everything I could, I really did. You might not think I care, you probably think what I'm doing is selfish but I think this is the best thing I can do for you. I'm just a burden now, I'm not happy and I don't want you to think it's because of you I'm not happy. It isn't, I just don't know how to cope with life, it's too difficult for me, waking up every single day is difficult.

You've still got Mrs Smith, she will look after you until you get on your feet. She doesn't know I'm going away either. I can't face her, she's done a lot for both us and I'm too ashamed that I have let her down. She will be able to look after you much better than I ever can. You need to get on with your life without me and do all the things you've dreamed of. You're not going to be able to do that with me around. I will relapse soon, I might even have by the time you read this. I would rather leave than have you see me like that again.

When you were a kid I tried my hardest to cope but I didn't know how to. I didn't have any support, your father ran away and even though I have defended him all these years I've realised he wasn't a good person either. He was as much to blame as me. Don't ever try to find him, I don't think he would want anything to do with you. He will only break your heart and you've had enough of that in your life already. You need to try and get on the best you can without either of us, not that you've ever really had either of us.

The day you were born I looked into your eyes and knew one day you would make something of yourself, you would be successful, you would make me proud, you have made me proud. You are still fighting and you are still trying to do your best for yourself. I know you tried your best for me too but I'm not worth fighting for anymore. You can't keep living your life worrying about me. Just carry on with school and make something of your life. Don't ever give up and turn out like me, you're worth a lot more than that.

I don't know where I'm going myself, I'll find somewhere though. I won't be in contact with you, I don't want you to find me. I know that right now it's going to hurt you a lot, but I want you to carry on fighting. I know you won't ever forget me but please try and understand why I'm doing what I'm doing. Even if you do make something of yourself, if you end up with lots of money, I don't want you to try and find me. I don't deserve it and I wouldn't want it. Everything you achieve in life will be down to yourself and I had no part to play in it.

I'm a coward too. I couldn't face you to tell you this. I knew you would try and persuade me not to do it and I wouldn't be able to go through with it. I don't want to be persuaded not to do it. I just want to go and start somewhere else, away from everything and everyone. I couldn't face you either because I don't know if what I'm doing is the right thing or the wrong thing. Everyone will say it is the wrong thing to do but I really do think it's right. You don't need me anymore, I need you but it isn't fair.

This life isn't for me, I can't live like normal people. Don't worry because I always find a way to look after myself. I just want you to remember that even though I wasn't very good to you and that I failed at being a mother to you I still tried even though I didn't show it very well. I always loved you and only want what is best for you. Wherever I am and whatever I'm doing, I will always be thinking of you and how you are doing. Please look after yourself and don't worry about me, I'll be okay, I always am.

Love Mum

Karl Marx

"You asked that geezer about that job yet?"

"I did, mate, but he said he can't sort no one else out, just me, ain't many spaces. Sorry, I did ask him though."

"What's that? Like that time you said you was going to sort me out some tickets to go and see the football off your mate that knew some of the players?"

"Fuck off, Paul! I told you he didn't have any left, I tried for you like I tried to sort John out that job. John, you believe me don't you?"

"Yeah, I believe you."

I don't think he does though, he rolled his eyes as he looked at Paul when he was saying it. The pub is full, it's Friday night, they'll forget about it soon, we'll all be best mates doing stupid things before the owner kicks us out. I've been looking forward to Friday for once, I've told myself I need to get myself out more, try and make an effort, achieve small goals like that woman I go and see at the counselling told me I should. I've been listening a bit more to her, maybe she don't talk as much shite as I thought she did.

I know most of the people in here, I went to school with them, funny, they had nothing to do with me back then, I was the loner, now they don't really seem to care, you just know each other so you start up nonsense conversations. They all know my mum up and left me but no one mentions it, a lot of them have got their own problems or they just don't care. The old boy is still at the bar, surrounded by people but still not saying a single word. How do you end up like that? Maybe he wanted to, he might be like me, he just doesn't like other people. I swear he'll never die!

The tunes coming out of the jukebox are all 80s songs that no one really knows the words to but pretends to sing along like they know them. 'Come on Eileen…'. There's a couple of lunatics in the corner staring at people, wanting them to stare back. They're drinking orange juice, their Friday night isn't about getting pissed, it's just about finding someone they can have a row with. People coming out of the toilets rubbing their noses, like they have to show everyone what they've just being doing because no one else knows do they?

"What you lot doing after?"

"Was just going to go home."

"You need to start getting yourself out of that gaff a bit more, I don't know how you do it, I'd have gone mental by now."

"I'm here ain't I? I was in here with you the other day as well. I like my own company."

"I'm just saying mate, it can't be doing you any good. I'm going to some party afterwards, you fancy coming along?"

"Whose is it?"

"Some geezer my brother knows, it's in some flat over the way. Come over it'll be a laugh, I don't want to go on my own."

"Why don't you ask one of them if they want to go?"

"They're all going to some club but I'm skint."

"Go on, I'll go for a couple of hours, ain't really my thing though. What time we going?"

"About 1ish, there won't be anyone there until then."

I step outside for ten minutes, the pub is too smoky and I need some air. It's dark and the lights are on in most of the flats, there's a strange atmosphere about Friday nights around here. Half the people don't work, they could do this any night but Friday nights feel different. There's a buzz about the place, the lights from the windows give off a warm glow that they don't have on other nights, people seem happier and friendlier, talking to people they'd probably being talking about all week. I see the door to the old flat open and someone walk inside and the light go on, I turn and head back into the pub.

"When we off, John?"

"It's too early yet, what's the matter with you?"

"Nothing, we could go and get a few cans and go and sit in the park for a bit."

"We're not 12."

"It's just a bit stuffy in here, you can have a few spliffs if we're in the park, you can't do that here."

"Give me ten minutes, I want to get this bird's number."

"I'll go to the shop and buy a small bottle of vodka."

The park is empty, not even any alkies kipping on any of the benches. We walk over to the little hill where I used to sit when I was a kid, looking out over the big buildings in the city. It looks beautiful at night, there's even more buildings now than when I used to come here. John is rolling up a spliff, lost in his own thoughts, I pass him the small bottle of vodka and he takes a mouthful from it and hands it back to me, shivering at the taste of the cheap alcohol. He finishes rolling up and lights it up, inhaling deeply and loudly.

"What's it all about, Jay?"

"What you on about?"

"What's it all about? All this, you see all them buildings over there, they're less than a mile away, them people working in there are fucking rolling in money. Do you think they ever think about us lot living in the estate they can see from their nice big offices?"

"Why would they?"

"They ain't got no reason to, of course they ain't. They grew up always knowing they were going to do something with their lives, they had opportunities, man, who the fuck ever gave us opportunities?"

"We both went to school, we both fucked it off when we were 16, if we'd have tried we might have got somewhere, better than what we have anyway."

"You never had a fucking chance. Sorry mate, but you didn't. Your mum was a smackhead, you spent most of your time on your own trying to look after yourself while she was out selling herself to make money. "

"Still my choice though. They said I could have done things with my life, that English teacher was always saying I could go university, if I really wanted it I could have been a writer."

"That's bollocks, they was only saying that because they knew how rough it was for you. We're born with no opportunity, we were only ever going to turn out this way. My kids will be the same, their dad ain't got a job, he spends half his time in the pub and the other half in the betting shop losing all the money he has to look after them. Their mother sits around all day smoking herself to death and watching shite on television."

"Yeah but that's up to you though ain't it. You're choosing to do that. If you really wanted to you could get yourself a job somewhere. Your missus, she could too, but you've both got a victim mentality, you think everything has to be laid on a plate for you."

"If it's that fucking easy how come you ain't sorted your shit out, how come you still live here? You could have walked away if you wanted to. You said they offered you some flat somewhere else. When I was a kid, my old man, he used to batter my mum half to death. I had to watch that every day, scared shitless he'd come home drunk. I'm a victim of the way I've been brought up, I didn't fucking choose that. How was I supposed to get any confidence from all that? Things were shit, of course I feel like the world owes me something, it fucking does."

"I ain't saying what you went through wasn't bad, I know that. I chose to come and live here because I don't know anything else, I don't know how to live outside this bubble of people. You all used to laugh at me when I was a kid but you were all still my people, the ones I know and I feel comfortable with."

"So you agree with me? You're a product of your upbringing like your old lady was too, my old man was too. That's what I'm saying, no one gives a fuck about how we live, they'd rather we just get on with it, we don't have a fucking voice and they'd rather it was kept that way. It's fucking bollocks but what am I going to do about it? I'll go to the pub tomorrow and get pissed, go to the betting shop, put a load of money on a dead cert, lose it all and then blame everyone else."

"Whatever man, since when did you become Karl Marx?"

"Who the fuck is Karl Marx?"

"Don't worry about it. I agree with you but we've got to make our own choices sometimes, I come back here, but do I really want this? Not really, if I'm honest, I want to get out, I want to do something with my life."

"Whatever, you won't do anything, you'll end up like that old geezer in the bar that sits there all day drinking and not talking to anyone. Come on let's go, get to this party, been talking a bit too deep, it's not good for my head."

People are standing outside the flat the party is in, hanging around looking moody, like people are supposed to be intimidated, most of them are kids, probably still at school. Inside is filled with faces of people I don't recognise apart from one or two. John wonders off into one of the rooms, I go into the living room where there are a load of people sitting on the sofas watching some strange Japanese cartoon. No one is talking to each other, just sitting there watching something they can't understand.

I leave the room and see someone I used to go to school with.

"What's happening man, not seen you about for ages, what you up to these days?"

"Still living on Shakespeare, what about you?"

"Moved away up north, working in some factory, it's boring but I make good money, just come down for the weekend to see my mum."

"Yeah? Sounds better than being here, I'm writing a book, got a few publishers want to look at it, reckon it's going to be successful."

"Yeah, I remember you used to write a lot in school. What are these publishers saying then? You going to be famous?!"

"Yeah, it's looking like that, get famous and move away, live a good life."

"Listen I got to go, need to speak to someone, I'll catch up with you later."

He walks off and starts talking to someone else. I see them both look over at me and then start laughing, he does that thing people do with their fingers when they think someone is crazy, his finger against his head and turning it. I go into one of the other rooms, I see Kelly sitting on the floor, her eyes glazed over staring at the wall. There's two other people in there but they are in a worse state than she is, collapsed against the wall, eyes barely open. I sit down next to her, hoping she'll recognise me.

"What's happening Kelly?"

"What you doing here? Didn't think this would be your sort of thing."

"John asked me to come, how's Joe?"

"Don't know, not seen him since he fucked off to Spain and left us, he hardly phones mum."

"I'm sure he still cares about you."

She looks at me in disgust then picks up a piece of foil I hadn't noticed, brown streaks running down the fold. She burns the underneath of the foil and breathes in the smoke, turns away and blows it back out and leans against the wall.

"Why you doing this to yourself?"

"Fuck's it got to do with you? I didn't ask you to come in here, I was just chilling now you're fucking up my buzz."

The time I was sitting in their house, at the dinner table when she smiled at me and I turned bright red. The pretty girl that used to say 'hello' to me when she saw me outside, ask me how I was. That girl is gone, her face is pale and drawn, the venom in the words coming from her mouth, it's like I'm sitting here looking at my mother. I want to shake her, pull her up and drag her out of this house, but I know it wouldn't do any good.

"I ain't going to preach to you, if you ever need someone to talk to you know where I live, I ain't going to judge you, I won't tell you what to do."

"Why would I go and talk to you? Do you think people believe all the shit you come out with? John only hangs around with you because he feels sorry for you and he ain't got no other friends. You talk shit, everyone knows it, everyone calls you 'Liar'. If your mum did come back she'd probably fuck off again when she found out how you've turned out."

"You're sitting here out of your nut on heroin, you're going to start clucking in a few hours and you'll have to go and find some old man that'll fuck you so you can go and sort yourself out again. I do talk shit, I know that, I'm a fuck up, but then I look at you, I see my mum, you're exactly like her Kelly. Thing is, if you turned up at my door tomorrow morning asking for help, I'd do what I could. See you later."

The kids are still standing around outside looking moody, I barge past them, one of them tuts at me but doesn't follow. I don't really want to go home, I'll only drink myself stupid, not because of Kelly but because of who she turned into tonight. I walk towards the canal, stopping at a shop along the way to buy another small bottle of vodka. I find a bench to sit down on and open the bottle taking a long swig, gagging at the vile taste, I can feel the warmth though, that's what I wanted. I throw the bottle cap into the water, and lean back on the bench looking up at the night sky, cloudless, starry.

I know why I do it. I'm ashamed of myself, I don't want to be me, that's why I create this alternate reality, thinking people might respect me. They don't though, they just think I'm an idiot. I never used to do it much when I was a teenager, it was like the adversary was enough to give myself a story, the smackhead mum, living on my own for most of the time, all them things made me feel like I was someone, they weren't good things, but they were things that gave me a story. Since she left I've had nothing, just myself and a boring life.

What can I do about it though? John was right, how the fuck do I get out of this, I might just have been destined to end up like this, product of society's flaws and all that shite. I could write a book but who would look at it? I'll send it to a publisher and they'll just throw it straight in the bin. My story, that ain't the kind of story they want to hear. The kid at school who told me I should write it all down, I wonder where he is now? What has he done with his life?

Thing is, like I said to John, it is partly my fault. I had the opportunities, the things that affected me in life, my mum, not having a dad and all that shit, they didn't make me throw away school, I chose to do that, I could have carried on, kept fighting for what I wanted, but I was doing it all for her, I wasn't doing it for me. You can't keep fighting for something you don't want. What do I want now? I want to say I don't know, but that's a lie too, I do know, I want out of here, I want to try and achieve something. I need to stop being the victim.

I throw the half full bottle of cheap vodka in the canal and then instantly regret it, I'll have to get another bottle on the way back home if I can find somewhere that's open. An attempt at a gesture of a new start just makes me look stupid. I want to go home, start putting everything I've written down together, but I can't look at all of that stuff without having a drink. When the book's done I'll give it up for good, I don't really have a problem with it, I just need it to get me through this, the start of my new life.

Fuck it, I will give it a go, I told John he was a victim but I've been a victim for the last ten years of my life. He'll go down the bookies tomorrow and waste all his money on horses, I'll sit at home and write, I'll try and find out how I can do this. I feel better but I feel embarrassed too, what I'm aiming to do, is it just like one of those lies I tell? It sounds like something you'd see in one of those feel good films where the guy is all fucked up and then sorts himself out and everything is happy in the end.

I'm No Better than Her!

I don't know what to do anymore, I'm at my wits end. I don't know what I've done to her to make her turn out like this. I always thought I'd given them the best life I could, but I can't have. My son has moved away to a different country and my daughter has ended up a drug addict. All these years I used to blame everyone else for all the problems we have round here but now I can only blame myself. I'm the one that brought them up, I should have realised something was wrong before it got to this stage.

I ain't got no one else. I spent years looking down off that balcony and talking about everyone else and now I'm just like them. Maybe I'm worse because I judged them all. Now I've ended up all on my own. My husband is still a fat layabout who don't do nothing, I thought he did care but he doesn't do nothing, he just sits there feeling sorry for himself hardly saying a word. Surely he must look at Kelly and think about what he did wrong too? What he could have done to make her life better so she ain't ended up like this.

I used to look down at her, walking out of her door of a morning, looking like shit, not giving a fuck about that poor boy of hers. I used to think she was the scum of the earth, that she didn't care about no one but herself. I used to pity the kid, now I look at him all grown up and think that despite everything, he's done okay for himself, the one person we all thought was weak looks like he's the strongest out of all of us. I don't know how he coped, I don't know if he still is able to cope but it looks like he can. He must be coping better than I do anyway.

People always thought I was strong, that I was a tough, hard woma-n who had seen it all. I wasn't though was I? I was just like everyone else. I thought I was tough, I thought nothing would ever be able to bother me. Now my daughter is on drugs and I cry myself to sleep every night wondering whether she will be coming home or not, whether she'll still be alive tomorrow. All of it is my fault because I ain't looked after her properly, I was more worried about looking at other people and talking about what they were doing wrong and not thinking about what I did wrong.

I suppose Joe has done okay for himself. I shouldn't blame him for walking away from us all. He had the chance to get away and he took it. I should be proud of him but I find it hard. I know he made the right decision but I wish he was here, I wish he was able to talk some sense into his sister. She don't listen to me, she might listen to him. It feels like he's ran away from me, like he felt he didn't need me anymore. I've been left here all on my own to try and sort out all this mess and I don't know what to do.

I'm lonely, that's what it is. Like I said, I thought I was tough, but I ain't, being tough all these years means that now I ain't really got anyone, people don't want anything to do with me, they see me as that person who was standing on the balcony and judged them, told them how they should be running their lives. Now they probably look down on me, they probably pity me, talk about my daughter being a smackhead and my son having run away because he'd probably had enough of me. I can't really say nothing though, that's what I used to do.

Maybe it's me that needs to get away. How can I leave though? I'm the only one that's keeping Kelly alive. If I ain't here she'll give up, I know that. I don't care about my husband, I'd leave him tomorrow and not care at all. We're only together because that's how it has been for years. There ain't no other reason for us to be still together. We hardly talk to each other, we never go out anywhere together, ever since the kids grew up we ain't even gone down to the seaside together. Is it any wonder I'm lonely?

I only wish someone would talk to her, talk some sense into her. I just want my daughter back. Joe chose his own way, I can always see him if I really want to. I feel like I've lost my daughter though, the little girl that wouldn't stop talking when she was a kid ain't here anymore. I can't get her to talk at all. I remember when little Jay came round for dinner all them years ago and Kelly was so worried about him. She kept asking me if he was okay and what she could do to help him. Now it's like she's dead, she don't care about anyone, I can hardly get her to speak.

It's all I want. I just want my daughter back. I'm so sorry for all those people I used to judge, I never really knew what it was like, now I know what it's like, I'm so sorry. I really am truly sorry for the way I looked down on people, the way I judged them, thought I was better than them. I know what it's like now, and it's killing me every single day, I cry every day, I hate myself for not doing enough to help her, I hate myself for having lost my two kids. I'm lonely and I'm scared and I don't know what to do anymore.

Walk in the Forest

"What happened at that party? I haven't seen you since, it's been weeks ago."

"Wasn't enjoying it so I went home, too many kids there. I've been busy apart from that."

"Making movies?"

"Writing a book."

"Where you going with that bag?"

"Just taking a few things to the charity shop."

"Fair enough. I've gotta go mate, come down the pub one night."

"Yeah, laters."

I've been avoiding him since that party, I like the fella but he can get on my nerves sometimes. I have to go and meet my counsellor today but I'm not going to go. I'm going away for a few days, instead of going out I've saved up some money and rented a small cottage out in the countryside. Nice and quiet, I'll be able to do some work and go for a few walks. I'm a bit nervous, I've never really been away anywhere on my own before, stupid for a 25 year old man! I'm really excited though, feel like I'm going on an adventure!

Walking along the platform I look for an empty carriage on the train. The top on has no one except for a man in a business suit reading a big newspaper. I walk to the top of the carriage and sit down, looking up at the map trying to work out how many stops there will be before I get to where I want. About 10 I think. It's like being excited as a kid and wanting things to fast forward, just waiting for the beeping sound of the train doors closing is torture, I just want to get moving! They beep, the train hisses and starts moving.

This place I've rented is a little cottage, I've used up all of my money to rent it, probably won't be able to go out and get anything to eat while I'm there but I can just go to the supermarket and get some cheap stuff to cook. It's on the edge of a forest, there's loads of walks, I'd like to rent a bike but I don't know if I'll have enough money. We'll see, walking through the forest will be good enough. Reminds of when I used to dream of going to a forest full of animals when I was a kid! I've got butterflies in my stomach.

The train moves slowly while we're still in the city, all the buildings full of people working, people standing on platforms reading newspapers and looking important. I can see my block in the distance, it actually looks quite pretty in a strange way, the sun is low in the sky behind it. I wish I had a camera, that would look amazing on my wall if I could have it enlarged. I don't think I appreciate the place enough, not just the estate, the whole city, when I come back I should start exploring it a bit more.

The buildings start turning into fields, the trees are bare, the fields are still covered in a frost, it looks beautiful. I love the cold weather, especially when you're inside and looking out at it. The train pulls into a station, there's nobody on the platform, the man in the suit gets up and leaves the train. Where's he going? I didn't think he'd be getting off in the middle of nowhere. Maybe he lives out here. Are we there yet? Only another eight more stops to go. Never had the chance to say that when I was a kid so might as well say it now!

I open up my bag to make sure I have everything in there I need. It's the third or fourth time I've checked. As long as I've got money and clothes it doesn't matter. What if I didn't go back? If I just left? Would I have enough stuff to keep me going until I got myself sorted? I could do it if I wanted to. I'd have to tell Mrs Smith though, it wouldn't be fair to just leave her without saying anything. The further away I am the more I feel like I don't want to go back and I'm only sitting on the train. We'll see.

I take out my pen and paper, looking out of the window I try to think of something I can write about. Some of the fields are covered in reddish, brown leaves. There's a man in one of the fields walking with a dog, a brief glimpse of him as the train passes. I wonder if that's his field? Someone like him would make a good story. I start to write, I feel good, I look up again and out of the window smiling, I feel positive, it's amazing how just a small change, an hour away from home can completely change your mood.

The driver speaks over the announcement thing. The next stop is mine. I put my book and pen into my bag and try to find the map I've brought with me. There it is. I look over it, remembering the route I have to take when I get off the train, I want to try and find it without looking at the map again. The doors open and I step out onto the platform, it's empty, no one else has got off the train. The air is so crisp, I breathe heavily just so I can see the small white cloud come out of my mouth. Still smiling, anyone watching me from the train will probably think I'm a nutcase.

The woman said on the phone the key will be under a rock just outside the door. That can't be very safe? What if the key isn't there? What will I do then? I'll work something out, for once in your life stop worrying about every little thing and enjoy yourself. I turn out of the station on to a road that doesn't look like it could fit more than one car on it. It should be at the bottom of this road, about a mile down it she said. I have gone the right way haven't I? It's definitely the right way, she said there's a large tree that has fallen over opposite the cottage, I can see it.

It's strange how quiet it is, I haven't seen a single person, there wasn't even a ticket inspector at the station. There looks to be a cottage not too far ahead on the other side of the road, that must be it, there aren't any others around. Blue door with a thatched roof she said, it looks blue from here. My heart is racing, this is my new home for three days! I see a rock next to the door and pick it up, there's the key. You wouldn't be able to do that back home. I notice there's a path to the side of the house that seems to head off into the forest, I'll have to have a look later.

Inside the cottage the walls are made from stone, there's a living room, a door to the kitchen and another door to a small bedroom. Next to the bedroom is a tiny bathroom. How do I turn on the heating? It's freezing in here! I see there's a fireplace with wood stacked next to it. How am I supposed to use that? I open the door to the bedroom, the bed looks warm, I shouldn't really lie down, I'll be wasting time. A little rest won't hurt, I get under the blankets, I can still see my breath in the air. I close my eyes for five minutes.

I've not slept like that for years. No bad dreams, I feel like I've rested. I get up out of the bed, I had better change my clothes. I should get something to eat too, where will I get that? I thought there would be more near here, it looks like there is nothing. I go into the kitchen and open the fridge, there's a load of food in there. Bacon, eggs, sausages, even a whole chicken. It can't be for me though? I'll have some and then put it back when I find somewhere to buy some food. Bacon and egg sandwich.

Best sandwich I've ever had! I take out all my clothes out of my bag and leave the pen and paper in it. I don't need anything else. I look out the window. The sun is still shining, it's only 2 in the afternoon. Out the door and down the path to the side of the house. I didn't even change my clothes, what's wrong with me, I'm like a little boy. I keep following the path through the forest, the trees are a red colour, I've never seen ones like it before. I reach an opening, it looks like someone has built a fire in the middle of it, could you cook something on it? I could take that chicken down here tonight and make a fire. I don't know how to start one though. Probably best I don't, I could end up burning the whole place down!

I want to find somewhere to sit for a little while, even if it is really cold. There's a path leading down and one leading up, I take the one going up the hill. At the top there's another opening, I can see out over the tops of the trees. Past the trees there looks like there's a little village, I must be able to buy a few things there. That will be my adventure for today, it doesn't look too far away and one of these paths must lead to it. I sit down on the damp grass, this is spectacular, how can a place so beautiful be so close to home? Maybe I should just stay out here.

Down the hill again, at the bottom I take the path which looks like it's going in the direction of the village. I keep looking around me to see if I can see something I haven't seen before, everything is so new. With no leaves on the trees it looks like one of them paintings you see on people's walls, all it needs is a bit of snow to cover them and I would really be in a painting. I hear something call out, it sounds like a bird but I've never heard anything like it before. I sit on a log that's beside the path listening but it doesn't come again, as I walk, I look up at the trees to try and catch sight of whatever made the sound.

The path comes to a road, the sky is starting to become a pale blue, it'll be dark in an hour. I can see a couple of houses and a pub. I walk down to the pub, there are a few people inside, I keep walking past it, I want to go in but those old fears hit me, I'm scared, everyone will start looking at me when I walk in the door. The village is smaller than I thought, only a few houses and a post office that looks like a shop too but it's closed. I reach the end and turn back, I'm going to go into the pub this time, what does it matter if they look at you? This is your holiday.

I push open the door, an old man with a dog sitting at the bar turns as I walk in, he throws his hand up in acknowledgement, I smile but he's already turned back to his drink. It's hot inside. I walk up to the bar, no one else has taken any notice of me, the barman cheerfully asks me what I would like to drink, I tell him just a Coke. He laughs, shakes his head and pours the coke from a glass bottle. I hand him the money, I want to say something but I don't know what, just to be polite, I can't think of anything so I just sit at the bar.

"You staying in the cottage up the road?"

"Yeah, I arrived this morning. It's lovely here."

"It is, you're from London?"

"I am, yeah. How do you know?"

"Your accent. Strange time to come down here isn't it? It's a bit cold."

"I don't mind the cold, I just thought it would be a nice place to get away to for a few days."

"Well, you're welcome here while you're down."

"Thanks."

"What do you do up there in London?" What do I do? What do I tell him, he wouldn't know the difference whatever I tell him. What's the point in making things up?

"I'm a writer."

"Yeah? What have you written?"

"Not much, just a few short stories about the place I live in, a few things about places I'd like to go. I'm not well known or anything."

"One day, hey?"

"Hopefully."

"Here, have a pint on me, not often we get writers from London drinking in here!"

"Haha, thanks."

I sip the free pint slowly, just taking the place in. I hadn't noticed how old it is. The other people are talking to each other quietly, but they seem relaxed, the whole place just feels calm. It's like they have no worries, back home everyone always seems to have some kind of a worry. Go home or not? I don't have any money, that's the biggest problem, there's Mrs Smith too, but I could just write her a letter, she would understand, she wanted me to leave before. What about friends? What friends? They're just people I know.

If I just walked out the door now and kept walking would I be able to survive? This is the first time I've ever been anywhere outside of London on my own. Of course I'd survive. It always comes back to that problem though, money, I don't have any. Spend the rest of my life wandering, that would be cool, wandering and writing, watching people. I have to find a way to do it, I have to go back first. I don't want to, since I left home it feels as though a door has been flung wide open and there's brightness coming from everywhere. I didn't know I could feel content. I didn't even make anything up when I was talking to the barman.

I put my hand in my pocket and count my money, hopefully no one can see what I'm doing, finding pound coins and counting them. Enough for one more pint. The barman pours it and then goes to talk to the old man. Thing is, if I walk off, on my own, wandering, will I ever find anyone to wander with. I'm not scared of being on my own, but it would be nice to have someone. I'm not sure I want kids, there's a fear at the back of my mind that I wouldn't be able to bring them up properly, that I'd either run away or do things wrong.

Wishful thinking. I can barely talk to a woman let alone have a relationship with her. The time that girl from school stopped talking to me, pretending she wasn't in when I knew she was, that ruined my confidence. I didn't think I did anything wrong. I thought she was a nice person. I wonder where she is now? It doesn't matter, I've come here to get away from all of them thoughts, all of them people.

"You look deep in thought there?"

"Nah, I'm just thinking about a few things. I'll be off in a minute, better get back to the cottage before it's too late."

"You'd better walk along the road just keeping going straight and it's on your left, you'll get lost in the forest, the paths all look the same in the dark. You should come here tomorrow night, a few of the local lads come and play cards. Better than being stuck in the cottage on your own."

"I'll think about it, not sure what I'm going to do tomorrow but it sounds like a good idea."

I can't really afford it, I want to go though.

"You can have a few drinks on the house." He winks at me, "just don't tell anyone."

I'm smiling as I walk back down the road to the cottage. The path into the forest seems tempting, stupid but tempting. What's the worst that can happen? I'll get lost and just wait until the morning to find my way back. It's not as cold as I thought it would be. Go on, you don't get many chances to be a kid again. I leave the road and try to follow the path, I pretend I'm on an adventure, a kid lost trying to find his way home through the dark forest. It's supposed to be scary but I'm not, I can't be scared, I'm excited, I'm that 9 year old boy but this time there's no mother waiting at home and no kids to tease me.

Time to Let Him Go

I've noticed a difference in him recently, he seems more positive, it must have been that holiday. I'd been really, really worried, I could see him going down the same path his mother did. I think he's taking this writing business a bit more seriously, he's realised he's actually got a bit of talent. I really hope he doesn't waste it all. Some of them idiots he hangs around with in that pub are a waste of space, I know a lot of them take the piss out of him too. I can't tell him to not hang around with them, he's a grown man. He'll see for himself one day I suppose.

I haven't been feeling too well lately, keep getting pains in my chest and getting dizzy when I get up to do things. I haven't said anything to Jay though. I don't want to worry him, I'm not sure how he'd take me being ill. Sometimes I think I might be a bit of a burden on him, I don't want him to feel like he needs to stick around because of me, I wish he had taken a flat somewhere else when he had the chance, he really shouldn't have come back here, there's too many bad memories but there was no telling him.

I was thinking back there the other day, I remember pushing him around in a pram downstairs trying to get him to go to sleep. I don't remember where his mother had gone but I was looking after him anyway. No matter what I did he wouldn't go to sleep, he could say a few words and he kept pointing at things and saying them, I'd just laugh and tell him he was so clever. When we came back that night he still wouldn't go to sleep so I put a tiny drop of brandy in his bottle and he was out like a light. They were good times them, simple things that made me happy. You'd get arrested if you did that now.

I got a letter from his mum there a few months back, I haven't told him and I don't think I'm going to tell him. There's no point in making life anymore complicated. I used to love that woman like my own daughter but I don't think I can ever forgive her for what she did, I don't tell Jay, but it's how I feel. I don't care that she betrayed me, it was him she messed with the most. I keep meaning to tear it up and throw it in the rubbish. I'd let him make the decision like I did with his dad but I don't think this is a decision he can make a good choice on.

I think I'm going to treat myself to a small drink tonight after I remembered that story about the brandy. I haven't had one for years. That's one of the things I miss, being able to go down the pub and have a few drinks but there isn't anyone in there these days I'd know and even though I try and pretend that I'm not frightened of anyone, I don't want to walk back on my own. I know Jay would take me home but I really don't want to put him out, it isn't fair.

I remember one night when I was with Sarah's mum and we both got drunk and started to walk along the cars at the bottom of the blocks. People were shouting out their windows at us and started saying they were going to phone the police. They were good times them, didn't really care, sometimes wish I'd appreciated it a bit more. Oh well, not much I can do now. I should go to the doctor though, I don't think it's anything serious but these pains can't be too good. I'll go next week I reckon.

I've not told Jay but I've written a will that's leaving everything to him. I don't have much money but it'd be enough for him to go and do something he'd like to, maybe take a holiday or something or let him have a go at this writing business he keeps going on about. I don't know why I'm being so morbid lately, I could have another 20 years left in me yet! I've been thinking of giving him half the money and then he can get the rest when I go. He's a good kid, I'm sure he won't waste it, well I hope he won't anyway, not like that idiot John he knows!

I hope he comes round to cook me my dinner later. I might have a kip waiting here while he goes and does whatever it is he wants to do. I feel a bit tipsy after that brandy, probably wasn't the best idea to have one in the afternoon. I hope he'll be able to wake me up when he gets back otherwise he'll be carrying me up the stairs!

Linda

Joe's mum doesn't look like the frightening woman I used to see on the balcony. She looks tired and old.

"Thanks for coming, I wasn't sure if you would or not."

"Of course I'd come, why wouldn't I?"

"You haven't spoken to Joe in years…"

"Doesn't matter, you were good to me when I came round."

"What can I do about Kelly?" Why do people think I can solve their problems? I know I've experienced it with mum but I don't have the answers, if I did she'd probably still be here.

"I don't know what you can do. I'd say be there for her but I don't even know if that is going to have the outcome you want. Have you tried to talk to her?"

"Of course I've tried talking to her, she won't say nothing. I don't know what's wrong with her. I thought I'd brought the two of them up well and now look, Joe lives in Spain and never comes to see me and Kelly is on drugs."

I don't really want to be here. She saw me when I was out for a walk the other day and asked me to come for a cup of tea. Since I've come back from the cottage all I hear about are people's problems and how miserable everyone is. Is that hypocritical? I should at least listen to her.

"I don't have a magic answer for you, honestly, if I knew I'd help but last time I saw her she was really nasty to me, I'd rather have nothing to do with her."

"Please, just try and talk to her."

"Why me? I hardly know her."

"Well you know everything about it…"

"About what? Just because my mum was a junkie, it doesn't make me an expert."

How have I got myself into this situation?

"Just try…"

"Where is she?"

"She's in that flat at the top of the tower block she's always going to…"

"I'm not going to any crackhouse looking for her. If she comes home let me know and I'll think about it."

"Thank you, love."

"It'll probably do nothing."

"Can I ask you something?"

"You'll ask anyway so go on…"

"Have you ever heard from your mother?"

"Nope, nothing, not even a letter, I have no idea where she is."

"Don't you ever wonder what's happened to her?"

"All day every day I wonder what's happened to her. I want to say I don't give a fuck because she upped and left me one day but I do. Even if she's dead I'd at least like to know."

"We were good friends when we were at school you know?"

"How comes she ended up hating you?"

"We fell out, she turned a bit strange, hanging around with the wrong people. I don't know why she changed so much, it was odd."

"Yeah, listen I have to go, I'd rather not talk about her."

"She weren't that bad a person you know…"

I shake my head and walk out the door. What was all that about? At the bottom of the stairs there's a little kid kicking a ball against a wall. I feel sorry for him playing on his own, then two of his mates appear from one of the bottom flats and they run of towards the green. If someone gave me the chance to be a kid again, live a different life, would I take it? I'm not sure, I've started to think differently. Being the victim wasn't getting me anywhere. I wouldn't be me as a kid again but I don't think I'd be another kid either.

I have to go and see Mrs Smith. I open the door with the key she's given me, why didn't she give me one years ago? Maybe she didn't really trust me. Nah, that's stupid, I know she trusts me. She's sitting in the arm chair reading a newspaper.

"Get us a cup of tea will you love?"

"Yep, you okay?"

"Yeah, I'm fine, just being lazy."

"Remember that woman who was always on the balcony being nosey and shouting at people, the kid I hung around with for a bit when I was in primary school, his mum?"

"Oh yeah..."

"Just went round her house, she wants me to talk to her daughter about giving up drugs. I don't know what I'm supposed to say to her."

"Don't go if you don't want to."

"I'll see. I feel bad for not helping her but I don't want to get involved."

"You can't help everyone, if it doesn't feel right don't do it."

I hand her the cup of tea, her face grimaces as she adjust herself in her chair, it seems to hurt her when she moves. I sit down too.

"I was looking through some old stuff the other day. When you gave me my dad's address and I went down there, I took a flower from a flower pot on their window, it was really stupid, I don't know why I did it, anyway, I put in a book and I found it the other day."

"Did you ever go back again?"

"No, never felt the need to. I just seemed to let go of him, maybe everything with mum took over. I don't even think about him at all these days."

"What did you do with the flower?"

"Threw it in the bin, I felt embarrassed looking at it."

She just smiles while sipping her tea.

"If I left, what would you do?"

"I'd be happy for you. Where you going?"

"I don't know, I just want to get up and leave but I don't have the money. I'm trying to get a job."

"Don't think about me, just do it when you can. They'll get someone to look after me, just make sure you come back every now and again."

"I will. Are you okay now? I need to go, I forgot, I have to meet someone in half an hour."

"Yeah, but will you run round some milk this evening, I don't have much left."

"Yep, look after yourself, I'll be back later, I'll make you some dinner if you want."

Shit! I knew there was something I had to do. I told John I'd meet him in the pub, said he had a way of making a few quid for me. It's probably going to be some wild plan that'll never come to anything but I'm desperate. All I've been doing since I've come back is dreaming about heading away on adventures around the world. I even bought a lottery ticket the other day, I never do that, I should go in the shop and check it.

I pass our old flat on the way to the pub. The door is green now, I don't feel so bad passing it, how can such a small change make a big difference to the way you feel? The chip shop has gone, Georgie sold it and went back to Greece or wherever it is he's from. I miss him, he talked a lot of shit but he had a good heart, he knew what he was doing when he kept me talking in there when I was a kid. I never really thanked him properly, how would I be able to look him up? He wouldn't have told anyone where he lives.

John's sitting in the corner of the pub. He looks shiftier than usual. It's all the same old regulars in there.

"What you looking so moody about?"

"What you on about?"

"What's up? You said you had some way of making some money."

"Yeah, but I don't think you're going to be up for it."

"Why's that?"

"Don't know, just reckon you won't be."

"Well tell me then..."

"I've got some gear. If you can get rid of it for me I'll give you half the money."

"Yeah, you were right, I ain't getting involved in any of that foolishness. Where did you get it from?"

"You don't want to get involved so I ain't telling you."

"Fair enough, I should have known this'd be a waste of time."

"Come on mate, one time, you'll have a load of dough, you can fuck off and do whatever it is you want to do, write your book."

"Where did you get it from?"

"I'm not telling you, just get rid of it for me."

"Why can't you get rid of it? I don't know why you're getting me involved."

"There's thousands for you to be made here."

"I ain't doing it."

"I always knew you were a mug, you're full of shit, I bet your mum never did half the shit you said she did."

"I never said she did anything, it's always been other people that talk about me and her. If you want to sell gear, sell it yourself, I'm not on some moral crusade here, I just don't want anything to do with that shit. You're the mug."

Have I done the right thing by walking out? That was money right there. Enough money to just get up and go, do what I want. I slow down, should I go back? Wait, I still don't know why he wanted me to sell it. I don't even know anyone to sell it to. Nah, I'll leave it alone, it's not going to lead anywhere but trouble. The money though, you can find someone to sell it to no problem. Thousands of pounds and you can walk away forever. Nah, fuck that, there's something wrong with all of this, I'll end up getting nicked.

I stop outside the old flat. Look back at the pub, something is trying to pull me back in there. I see John walk out the door and into one of the other blocks. Nothing I can do now, he's gone. Could still go round his house. What's so wrong with it anyway? I'm not getting into a moral debate with myself. Just walk away, stay away from him. Go to Mrs Smith's and cook her some dinner, do anything but don't go home on your own because you're going to go looking for him. I need a drink, I just had the chance to change my life and I blew it.

The shopkeeper looks happy for once, what's he got to be so happy about? I give him a fake smile. What am I taking it out on him for? I give him the money for a beer and then go towards the building we used to live in. It's starting to get dark, I walk up the stairs to the top of the building and stand on the highest balcony. It doesn't look as good as I thought it did when I was a kid. I chuckle to myself, why did I just get angry? Some other opportunity will come along. I always wanted to come up here when I was a kid but I don't know why I didn't.

I look down at the green, there's still some kids kicking a ball about. If I had been like them when I was a kid, going out and playing football or just being normal, would I be trying to do what I'm doing now? Or would I just be happy with what I would have had? Her running away might have been the best thing that ever happened to me. I don't even want to be a well known writer, I just want to do what I love to do, tell stories, see all those places in the atlas that I dreamed of as a kid. I sigh and then laugh to myself again. I'd better go and sort dinner out.

Her flat is silent, not even the sound of the tele. She must be asleep, she sleeps a lot in the evenings these days. I turn the kitchen light on and shut the door. I can see the outline of her body on the armchair, it's cold, she must have forgotten to turn the heating on. I look up at the kitchen clock, it's 5 already. I'd better wake her up. I turn the living room light on, I know as soon as I see her, she's dead, I can just tell. She isn't breathing, I put my hand over where her heart is and feel nothing, I don't know if that means anything. She's definitely not breathing, she's gone. If I hadn't gone to see that idiot would I have been able to save her?

I sit down on the sofa. I'm shocked but I don't feel sad. She's gone but she was always there for me when she was here, I can't be angry, she's the only person who ever looked after me. Now what? I really do have to go, there is nothing here at all for me. I'd better phone an ambulance, she's dead though, do I still phone an ambulance? Who else can I phone? I pick up the phone, tell the woman I think my gran is dead. She might as well have been my gran. She says there's an ambulance on it's way.

I sit back down and wait. It's all going through my head, the last 25 years, the times I used to come here as a kid, the time she gave me the address to find my dad, when we would sit and talk for hours and hours.

"Mrs Smith, I know your name is Linda, I just always called you 'Mrs' out of respect. I've always respected you. I never told you before and I know you can't hear me now, but I need to say this out loud because most of my life I've been bottling everything up. You really were my mother, you looked after me when she wasn't there, you came to see the teachers at school because she couldn't be bothered. I hope I showed you enough gratitude and you knew what you meant to me. I was thinking earlier, I saw a little kid kicking a ball and I thought of myself when I used to wait outside the flat while she was seeing geezers inside, would I take the chance to be a different kid. I wouldn't because if I did you wouldn't have been a part of my life. I don't know what I'm going to do now, there's no reason for me to stay here, I just have to find some way of getting some money together to get away. You were the one person who never judged me and I thank you for that. All my life people judged me on my mum, on me not having a dad, that I made things up because I felt so insecure I felt I had to. You were the only person I could talk to properly, and be myself. Thank you, I'll miss you, this will be the hardest loss I've had to take."

Karl Marx Gets Banged Up

If that little prick had just taken that gear off me I wouldn't be in here. Of all the people I know I would've thought it'd be him that'd take it off me and go and sell it. What's the matter with him? He goes around talking shit all the time, I give him an opportunity and he mugs me off. I'm one of the only people that'll hang around with him and he still shows me no gratitude. Wants to be a writer? He ain't ever going to be a writer, he'll end up in some mental health place or be just like his mum.

There's a geezer in the cell next door crying, he must be drunk or something. Every ten minutes he starts screaming and they just ignore him. This isn't looking too good really, I'll end up going down for quite a long time. What is she going to do with the kids if I'm not there to look after them? She's ungrateful too, doesn't realise what I've been trying to do to give us a bit of money. All she does is moan about me being in the pub or the bookies, she don't moan when I win something though does she? Might be doing me a favour to go inside for a bit.

Last week she said to me that if I didn't get myself a job she was going to throw me out of the flat. How's that for appreciation? Where am I supposed to go? All she does is sit there in front of the tele smoking fags and drinking coffee and I'm out all day trying to come up with ways to make money. I knew I should have left her years ago. It's her fault as well, if she didn't put me under so much pressure I wouldn't have been stupid and tried to help her brother out. She better realise it's her fault.

It was her brother as well, come over said he had a load of gear he wanted to get rid of, reckoned I could pay him back once it was gone. I thought this is an easy way to make a few quid. He's going to want his money now, and fuck knows where he got the gear from in the first place because they're going to want their dough as well. Ain't my problem, I don't care what happens to the brother, I never liked him anyway. I might just grass him up, if I'm going down I'll take him down with me.

When I come out of the pub I knew I should have just gone straight home. I went to that crack house instead where that big geezer that I always see around sells his gear from. He always used to be outside Jay's house when his old girl was round. That's why I wanted him to take it, I thought he'd be able to sell it to that geezer. Go in there and it's filled with crackheads, place was filthy, two minutes later and there's Old Bill everywhere. They nicked everyone and I had all this gear in my bag. Bang to rights.

Yesterday when I was in the bookies I knew something bad was going to happen. Every horse I backed come in last. All my dough was gone, when I come out of the betting shop I went into the pub and asked one of the others if they could sort me a pint and they all said they was skint. To top it all off, when I come out of the pub there was a magpie on the green. Just one of them, I was looking everywhere for another one and couldn't see it. I should have known then that things were going to go all fucked up.

If he hadn't made things up about jobs I wouldn't be here. Telling me I could get a job as an extra in a film. I was stupid enough to believe him as well. See, if he didn't tell me that, I could have gone out and got another job and then when her brother come around I would have just told him to do one. How do I meet these people? Taking advantage of a man just trying to look after his family. When I get out I'll go looking for him and sort him out.

Bye Bye

Looking through all these books I don't know what I'm going to do with them. I'll just give them to the charity shop I think. There isn't any trace of anyone else that was close to her. All these years and I never questioned or thought about how lonely she must have been. There are cupboards full of photographs and I don't know who any of the people in them are. I feel like I never really knew her, it was always about me or mum, never about her, now I realise that we were all she had too and I don't think we showed her enough appreciation.

I put another couple of black bags on the landing outside the door, how am I going to be able to get all of these down to the shop? There'll be a few more to go as well. Some of it is just going to have to be thrown out. I'll have a look through the couple of bedside tables as there might be something important in them. I open the first on up, there's a few more photographs, one of them must be her with the fella she went to New Zealand with, she's smiling in the picture, it must have been when she first got there.

Underneath the pictures there are a couple of old letters, I don't really want to read them, it feels a bit intrusive. I flick through the pages, there's one piece of paper that is still white and not the yellowish colour of the others. I take it out, curious as to who would have been writing to her recently. I know the handwriting. It's mum. It's dated from six months ago. Maybe it isn't her, handwriting just looks the same, I look at the bottom. It's signed Sarah. Why did she not give this to me?

Dear Linda,

I'm assuming you are still at the same address and you'll know how to contact Jay, you probably wouldn't have expected to get this after all these years. I never said goodbye to you before I left because I knew you would try and persuade me otherwise. I made a stupid decision that I've regretted ever since. I've not been in contact before because I was too ashamed and I didn't think either of you would have wanted to hear from me.

I've been clean for seven years, I live not too far outside of London although I did wander about when I first left. I live on my own but I have friends and support, none of them know about my past apart from one person and it's been her that has helped me build up the confidence to write this letter. Most of the fear is you'll not reply, if you don't I will understand, I would appreciate it if you could pass the letter on to Jay though.

I've taken responsibility for all the mistakes I've made, especially the biggest one which was running away and leaving him. I'm not going to write down excuses or reasons why I did it, there aren't any excuses. My life has changed considerably, I've even started an Open University course and I have a stable job. For years I've wanted to know how he is doing and what he is up to, I wish I could change what I did but I can't. I would just like the chance and the opportunity to start again now.

I want to say thank you to you to for all the help you gave me when I was growing up and all the help you gave me with Jay. I'm sorry for not letting you know where I was going, it was stupid but I can't change that now. If

you could please at least pass this on to him I would be grateful. My
address is at the bottom so he can contact me any way he likes.

Sarah

How come she never gave it to me? I trusted her and she never gave me
this letter. All this time spent wondering where she'd gone, and she knew
how much it hurt me but she didn't give me the chance to find out. I read
the letter again, make sure it is real, that it really is mum who wrote it. It
is. It definitely is. I sit down on her bed and let out a long sigh, I can't be
angry with Mrs Smith, she was only protecting me. What do I do with this
letter now? It's there in front of me, her address, I could go there now.

I fold up the letter, I'm just going to get rid of everything else, there's
nothing I can do with it. I put it all into black bags, a big pile of them now
outside the door and blocking the way, the council will sort the rest out.
As I go to shut the door, I look in one last time, remembering all the time I
spent here, those happy times when I came after school, the time I lived
here when mum left. I smile to myself

"Goodbye, Mrs Smith, I understand, I don't hate you for not giving me the
letter."

I move the bags to the shoot and throw them down one by one, I can't be
bothered to take them to the charity shop. Oh shit, the books, I can't
leave them in the rubbish. I race to the bottom and peer into the big silver
bin. I can see the bag with the books, I reach in and take them out. The
bag has all the books I read the most in it, I'll take them home to see what
I can do with them later. As I pass Joe's mums block she looks down at me,

I wave but she ignores me. Annoyed because I didn't go and see Kelly. Other people's problems aren't mine anymore, fuck them.

I put the books down on the floor in the bedroom, go into the living room and look out the window. I ain't going to be here in 20 years' time. I look down at the green, there's a kid kicking a ball about, there'll always be some kid down there kicking a ball about. His mate's join him and they start a game. I look across to the other flats opposite, people doing whatever it is they do in their kitchens, people sitting in their living rooms watching television. I hated it when I was a kid but if it wasn't for this place would I ever have made it this far? I don't think so, hard but I've learned from it.

I sit down at my desk. Just my pen and paper, no booze. I don't need it and I don't want to go down the road I was going. I'm happy, content. When that letter was first in my hand my first reaction was anger but it's gone away now. I know where she is, I can find her. Mrs Smith didn't mean anything bad by it all. I look at the address on the letter, I'm pretty sure you can get a train out there from here, wouldn't take too long. Would I recognise her now? She probably looks completely different.

I write, my emotions are different. The anger I used to write with is gone, the need to escape is gone. I finish what I'm writing and leave it on the desk. I pick up an envelope and read the letter inside one more time. I found it in Mrs Smith's drawer. She's left all her money to me, it isn't much but it's enough. I read it one last time with a smile, she never said she had any money, no reason to tell me I suppose. I do some calculations in my head, I've probably got enough of my own money to start off until hers goes through to my bank account.

I put the two letters into my bag and put it on top of my bed, take my jacket and walk out the door. At the bottom of the steps I stop and look over at the row of shops where the chip shop used to be, I used to love the warm feeling inside his shop. I carry on walking, heading towards the park, I stop briefly where I used to sit as a kid and look out at the buildings and all the lights, I go back out of the park and past the school and the small woods. I'm not brave enough to walk through them now, they don't look as big as they did then though.

Back home I pick up the bag of books and put them on my small bookshelf. I don't want to give them away. I take the atlas and lie down on the bed, look through all the maps. I look at the map of England and look up where mum lives. She was so near all this time. I rest the book on my chest and close my eyes, thinking of exotic places, thinking of all the people I've known and what they're doing now. I wince when I think of Joe's mum, I should have helped her talk to Kelly. I'm sure she'll find her own way.

Joe, what sort of a person is he now? He was the one who caused half the problems I had. If he had never told anyone I was making things up I probably wouldn't have had half the problems I had in school. That's a lie though, I would have. Kids are cruel and I was an easy target. There's no point in hating someone, if things had been the other way around I might have done the same. I think I still have that picture he drew for me. Sleep.

The sun wakes me, I forgot to draw the curtains before I fell asleep. I get up and make some coffee and eat a sandwich. I put what I wrote last night into an envelope and write an address on it and put it back into my bag. I go back into my room and pick up the atlas, it's too big to fit in my bag but I don't want to leave it here. I think it'll just fit in, might be a bit heavy but I can't leave it. I remember the picture I was thinking of last night, I open a drawer and look through the bits of paper, it's at the bottom, I put it into the atlas.

I look out the window one more time, it's too early for people to be about doing things. I wipe away a tear from my eye and pick up my bag. I look around the room one more time to make sure I have everything I need. It's all there. Out the door and down the stairs, I don't look back up at the flat, it wasn't really home, it was just a place I lived in for a while. Joe's mum is on the balcony smoking a fag. I walk over to her block and up the stairs. She looks at my bag and then smiles at me.

"I know why you didn't come that day, it wasn't your problem, I was just desperate, I didn't know what to do. She's home at the moment, she's sick but she says she wants help. She's said it before but hopefully this time will be different. Where you going with the bag?"

"Just going out, you look after yourself, look after her as well, I'm sure she'll be okay."

"I should have helped you more when you was a kid you know, I really should have done. Spent half my time thinking how bad everyone else was and it's come back to bite me ain't it?"

"I know where mum lives. She sent a letter to the old girl, I found it when I was sorting through her stuff."

"You going to go and see her?"

"We'll see. Listen, take care of yourself."

"Look after yourself Jay, pop round whenever you like."

Back down the stairs and over to the old flat. That place was home, it wasn't a good home but it was still home. Strangely I don't feel any emotion, I thought I would, if anything I feel relief. Time to go, finally get out of here. I look back one more time as I reach the edge of the estate and the main road. There's a small kid with a hood up walking past the row of shops, his head down. I look over at the old flat and there's a woman standing there watching the kid walk away, she waves but the kid doesn't acknowledge her, she looks sad as she closes the door.

Passing the post box I drop the envelope in and keep on going to the bus stop. The bus pulls up and I sit on the top deck watching the city go by, wondering when I'll ever see all of this again? I wonder what stories I'll have if I ever come back. They won't be able to say I'm making them all up then. I check the bag for my ticket and the passport I sorted out when I came back from the cottage. Going to go to a proper beach first and then wherever things take me. I hope I'll find that house in the middle of the fields one day, none of you ever thought I'd make anything of myself, but I will.

Dear Mum

Dear Mum,

Mrs Smith died last month, when I was looking through her stuff I found the letter you wrote to me. I don't know why she didn't give it to me but I'm guessing she was trying to protect me, she didn't want me to find you. I understand that, I hope you do too, don't blame her, she did a lot for us both. I finished clearing out her stuff today, it was sad, it's really strange not having her around, I'm sure if you get the chance you can go to her grave and say goodbye. She never really said much when you left, just tried to look after me, she was selfless and I hope you appreciate that.

When you left I didn't know what to do. The truth is, deep down I always expected you to relapse, I never had enough faith in you that you'd be able to keep going. I told myself you would over and over again but I knew. I didn't think you'd run away though, I thought I'd find you dead but never did I think you'd just be gone one day. The day I read that letter was the worst day of my life, no matter what you did before that I could have forgiven you.

Sitting here writing this I think back and I managed pretty well. Not ending up a complete fuck up was a good achievement. I know you thought leaving me was for the best but it wasn't, I could have coped with you around. I don't really understand why you haven't come to find me, I understand the shame and that you feel guilty but I think knowing you were clean for so long and still didn't come and find me hurts more. It wouldn't have been difficult.

When I was at school and all the other kids used to tease me about you I always stuck up for you no matter what. In the evenings I couldn't wait until I got home because I was hoping you were going to be there. I made this story up, I really, really wanted to tell you it. I was going to tell Mrs Smith but I changed my mind because I wanted you to be the first but you were never there, or if you were there you were in no state to listen to me. I've never told that story to anyone. It's something I'll keep there in my head to remind me of them times.

The kids at school used to call me 'Liar', I wanted to escape so much I created a new world for myself to escape into. I never told big lies really, they were just stupid stories. That name stayed with me, even up until now people still wonder if I'm telling the truth. It's partly my fault, I knew telling those stupid stories wouldn't be believed but it's your fault too, I had to create that other world because of you. When you left it got worse because I had nowhere else to go.

I don't hate you though, mum. I still love you. I don't think you can take the love for your mother away. I forgive you too, I know you couldn't cope and I do understand why you did what you did. I don't want you to feel guilty, guilt is a waste of time, you can't change anything that has happened so there's no point in tormenting yourself. I've finally learned to accept things, I hope you will be able to one day too.

Mrs Smith left me some money and I'm going away with the little bit of money that I have, when hers comes through I'm going to go travelling around the world. I don't know where I'm going to go, I haven't really thought about it, I just want to get away. I always said I wanted to write and that's what I'm going to do. The stories I used to tell were always for other people, because I wanted them to like me. The ones that I want to write will be for me, not for anyone else, I don't need other people to like me anymore.

I want to say that I'll come and see you one day or that I'll keep in touch but I'd be lying to you. Like I said, I don't hate you and I forgive you but I don't know if I still want to stay in touch with you or if I want you to be part of my life. That is something I'm going to have to work out. There's no address for you to reach me on anymore so don't bother replying to this. Remember that I love you mum, I always will, please look after yourself. Maybe one day I'll see you again, but now it's my time to live without your shadow over me.

Jay

Printed in Great Britain
by Amazon

27958246R00126